# Alligator Blood

India Vane

*For the readers who had to become their own heroes by slaying dragons in the form of those who were meant to protect you.*

# Alligator Blood Playlist

## Available on Spotify

- Poison Ivy - Hemi Moore

- Who Do You Want - Ex Habit

- Tip Toe - PatrickReza

- Let The World Burn - Chris Grey

- Make Me Feel - Elvis Drew

- Secrets - Omido, Ordell, Rick Jansen

- Hold On, I'm Comin' - Sam & Dave

- I Did Something Bad - Taylor Swift

- Gangsta - Kehlani

- You Don't Own Me - SAYGRACE, G-Eazy

- Him & I - Halsey, G-Eazy

- Ain't No Rest For The Wicked - Cage The Elephant

- Bad Karma - Miley Cyrus, Joan Jett & the Blackhearts

- Boys Wanna Be Her - Peaches

- Layla - Derek & The Dominos

- Way down We Go - KALEO

- Closer - Nine Inch Nails

- Money - Pink Floyd

- Change (In the House of Flies) - Deftones

- War Of Hearts - Ruelle

- A Little Death - The Neighbourhood

- Nothing's Gonna Hurt You Baby - Cigarettes After Sex

- Judas - Lady Gaga

- PRETTY PLEASE - Dutch Melrose, benny mayne

- i like the way you kiss me - Artemis

# Prologue

## Sonnet, 7th Grade

"Toughen up," Mom said to me with an eye roll while I sat on the kitchen table and held a bag of frozen peas to my cheek, trying not to cry. With one manicured hand on her hip, the other held a lit cigarette to the side so she could show me the full unobstructed extent of her disappointment. As the smoke from her Virginia Slims curled shapes slowly around the still ceiling fan above us, she made me explain for the third time how I spent another day slipping farther away from a daughter she could be proud of.

No matter how hard I tried, it seemed as though I was never able to reach the bar my mother set to continue the pageant queen legacy that meant so much to her. I'm sure it would have been easier if I hadn't been an only child, but from what she reminded me of constantly, she barely made it through a complicated pregnancy with me. I was officially her only chance at being a beloved pageant mom.

I restarted the story of the day's events that led me to the uncomfortable seat in the main office, my voice cracking as I held my tears inside. All I wanted was a quiet recess with the newest Dragon Princess chapter book I borrowed from the school library, but according to the royal court of popular girls in my class, it's not cool to like elves and their fight to control the dragonborn. I know Mom told me to ignore the bullies or simply not let them bother me, but when they ripped the book from my hands, I stumbled through my attempt at faking a show of strength. Loudly, I told them to shut up and leave me alone, but even through my feeble attempt at locating my backbone, they continued to laugh louder. Watching them take turns tearing the pages out, I couldn't help but get angry and for the first time in my life, I reacted.

When I shoved Jessica Turney backward, I braced myself for the immediate retaliation. When nothing happened, I thought maybe Mom was onto something about being too tough for them to pick on. My victory was short-lived. As I straightened my spine to walk away after defeating the girls that ruined the pages of what was on track to be my favorite book of the Dragon Princess Series, I felt a blunt and direct hit to my face. Cradling the shock and burning sting with both hands, I ran away before Jessica or her twin, Michelle, could get another slap in. When I made it inside the school, I pulled the heavy door shut and watched from the window to make sure I wasn't followed. All I saw were the pages of my favorite means of escape fluttering all over the ground.

"Those girls are just trying to get you to fit in," Mom told me with a nonchalant exhale of her cigarette and another exasperated eye roll. "You know, they're actually doing you a favor."

"It doesn't feel like they're being nice to me," I said with my brows drawn, looking up at my mother who probably wished she could trade me in for Jessica or Michelle since they would have loved competing at all ages for a crown and sash. Me on the other hand, I just wanted to read and imagine far away places only accessible by magic. I didn't see what was so terrible about that.

"Darling, the real world will chew girls like you up and spit you right out. Girls like *that* get the best husbands and the best jobs. *They're* set up for success," she explained as the bag of peas started to condensate and drip cold water down my face. I opened my mouth to tell her I didn't care about that stuff because I didn't even know if I wanted a husband when I got older anyway, but she didn't let me speak. "I told you to toughen up, not to pick a damn fight. You don't fight girls like that, you join them. Think about that, and don't give another sob story to your father. I'm sick of it."

I didn't say another word as she looked me up and down one more time before walking back to the living room to resume the show she'd paused. She always watched the news after her usual daytime talk shows so that when Dad came home from work, she'd make interesting conversation at the dinner table. I think she stays updated on current events in case somehow one day she'll return to the stage and nail the interview portion of the pageant she claims is the toughest to win. Since I got sent home early, she had to stop her routine to lecture me on the car ride back to the house about how I'd be responsible for doing additional chores to replace the book *I* allowed to be destroyed. I tried to protest and tell my side of the story, but she said that if I wouldn't have been so "weird and introverted" then I would have spent my time with *them* and not in a fantasy world. *Bookworms don't become queens*, she would always remind me. That's what she always got wrong though. My books are *exactly* where all the queens and princesses live.

After she was done lecturing me, I threw the peas back into the freezer and went upstairs to my room so I could read until it was time for dinner. Closing my door and quietly turning the lock, I pulled the small box from under my bed. I held the crown that I'd made with paper mache and painted to look exactly like how it was described in the first book of the Dragon Princess Series. When I looked in the mirror at the gold crown against my red hair, I momentarily forgot that I'm nursing an almost black eye from Jessica. If I was Althea, Witch Daughter of Lenore and Dragon Princess to the Gold Leaf Throne, I wouldn't hesitate to throw Jessica and Michelle straight to the hungry elves of Kansk.

When Mom called up for dinner, I hid my crown back in the shoebox under my bed with the playing cards Dad brought me back from all over the country, and the small seashell I found near the lake one summer that has what looks like a tiny fairy footprint in it. On my way out of my room, I took one more look in the mirror. I pretended I was just on another adventure where I had to hide my powers in plain sight knowing that if I was captured, I wouldn't be able to save my realm.

Even though I knew it was only pretend, it made me feel more powerful on days that showed me how cruel the world could be to those that are different or afraid to stand up. One day I'll be older and maybe when the time comes to be tough, I won't freeze or run away. One day, maybe I'll discover my power and fight back harder than anyone will ever expect. For now, I'll just dream about being an undercover princess while I eat the peas my face helped to thaw.

# CHAPTER ONE

## Sonnet

Hearing my mother's voicemail pick up for the fourth call of the day, I start to fidget with the anxious energy I'm usually better at quelling. It's been a stressful day in the ER, but as I'm sure any other hospital staff will attest to, the full moon brings out the chaos in everyone. We've seen food poisoning, a broken finger, a gash in need of stitches with a side of Tetanus shot, and chest pains that turned out to be terrible anxiety and indigestion. At least tonight I made it through a whole shift without getting one drop of bodily fluids on me, although with the gentleman suffering from food poisoning, it was a close call. If my reflexes were any slower, I would have been wearing Exorcist-themed scrubs set to celebrate Summerween. Sometimes I feel like I should have one of those signs that say how many days since there's been an accident just to see what it would look like. So far, the longest I've gone is four.

When my last patient during this shift is discharged, I check my phone one more time to see if Mom has called. No new notifications except for the few spammy push ones to alert me of a great new pizza delivery deal and free shipping on all clearance items on Zara. Shit. I rush through the break room to my locker to grab my purse, keys, and the latest annoying stainless tumbler everyone is obsessing over. I didn't need it, but there's a residual desire in my subconscious from my mother's lessons in popularity to latch onto trends, and hitch a ride on whatever bandwagon is rolling by. The only thing I could do to combat the buyer's remorse and tinge of identity loss was slap two fantasy romance stickers on it I bought for $4 off of Etsy that scream "I judge male fae by their wingspans" and "I'd let a blue alien hit it". *There*, I had said to myself, *now it looks like me.*

Even at 38, there are just some things that I refuse to compromise on much to the ire of a pageant parent who thought everything I liked was a phase. I still read incessantly, refused to obsess over marriage or even have any interest in one, and chose to tie my tubes at the ripe age of 22. After Mom tried to matchmake me with everyone's son from her Christian women's group, book club, and neighborhood watch meetings, she finally dubbed me the spinster she always feared I'd become. Nevertheless, despite our differences, when she was diagnosed with dementia a few years ago, I forwent my apartment lease and moved back home to save on nursing home costs.

Not thinking of anything but Mom not responding to my calls, I raced to my black Chevy Impala and hopped in to blast my AC as high as possible. Being inside the cold hospital, it was a shock to my body everytime I walked outside at the end of a shift in the summer. California was always beautiful, but damn the desert in those few triple digit months. Before I carefully back out of my reserved space, I turned the volume of my ringtone and alerts to the max so I wouldn't miss anything. I'm only a half hour from the house, but the quarter tank of gas nags me to stop telling myself I'll get to it later. It's one of the habits I know I'll break eventually, but I'm either rushing on my way into work, or I'm exhausted on the way home and assume I'll do it in the morning. Back and forth I play this game of chicken with myself and the small orange circle of light on the dash. *I'll do it tomorrow*, I decide.

My stomach growls when I reach the exit before my own, and on impulse I flip my turn signal on when I see the golden arches from the interstate. I'm worried about Mom, but no matter the reason for her not answering my calls, I'm sure she'll appreciate the cheeseburger and fries. I make sure to grab her a Diet Coke too since that seems to be one of the small luxuries she relies on daily, and everyone knows a crisp fountain Diet Coke is a universal cure-all. By the time I'm back on the road, I've already eaten a handful of french fries and awkwardly suctioned a few gulps of my thick chocolate shake.

At least the boost will give me the energy to handle whatever she'll be mad about today. The doctors warned me that the side effects of progressing through dementia are different for everyone, but that it can make her more easily agitated when she gets confused. They were right. She's already told me countless times that she wishes she could have traded my life for my Dad's since his heart attack was over a decade ago, but she hasn't been the same since. Every time she waves her crooked finger at me to remind me of her resentment, which I don't need since I'm painfully aware, I have to take into account her cognitive decline and lie to myself that it's the disease talking, and not her.

When I pull into the driveway, my fries and shake are gone and I've yet to finish my cheeseburger since I dropped a glob of ketchup on my scrub top and decided it was a sign to wait. So much for one day without staining my work clothes. While I wait for the garage door to lift, I see the package on the front doorstep and I rejoice in the small delight that is book mail. When I park and turn off the car, I notice the curtains don't move, meaning Mom isn't watching to see whose car just pulled in like she usually does.

Gathering everything in my hands, I almost drop my keys as I fumble for the pink-topped copy I have for Mom's house, but I freeze when I get to the door. It's open, leaving a three inch crack that you'd never notice if you were just driving by. All at once, dozens of worst case scenarios and horror movies pop into my head while I try to work out what to do.

*Is someone in there waiting for me?*
*Did I not close it the whole way when I left in a rush this morning?*
*If I left through the garage, who opened the door?*
*Has someone broken in to steal anything?*
*Is Mom in there being held hostage?*

Slowly, I approach the door and bend down to put the bubbled envelope in my bag. I pause to listen before kicking it gently with my foot. It creaks open to reveal the living room with the tv stuck on a screen that asks if I'm still watching, and all of the lights on. Walking in farther, I leave my purse wrapped with one handle on each knob so no one can shut it behind me. I grip my keys in between my fingers like Wolverine and hold my phone close to my ear while I carefully enter the living room. The remote is on the coffee table as well as the cordless landline Mom insisted upon us keeping, but so is her iPhone. There's a glass of water that must have started as ice water leaving a puddle around the base, and the AC is working overtime from the door letting the early summer air in.

"Mom!" I shout when I try to put the pieces together in my head. I rush toward the garage door in the kitchen and when I open it, I see the space where my car sometimes sits and her red Mustang. At first, it's always a concern that she would forget that she's no longer able to hold a license. We decided that as long as I stored the keys in an undisclosed location, then the car would stay as a memory of Dad only and we wouldn't have to get rid of it. Thankfully the car was still there, and I continue to call her name around the house as I peek in every room to find her.

When I realize that the house is completely empty, I put the facts together in my mind like a riddle and the clarity of the situation is heart wrenching. It's something I tried to avoid thinking about for a long time, but unfortunately it seems inevitable. Walking back to the kitchen, I set everything down before unhooking my purse from the door knobs. I unlock my phone and reluctantly dial 911 knowing that there's really only one likely explanation for this. As the dispatcher tells me that local police are on their way, I sit on the couch while the sun sets and try to process everything that's happened, is happening, and might happen in the very near future.

Within 20 minutes, there are two kind male officers at my door. They're both wearing wedding rings, and I think to myself that if Mom was here to see them, she'd be disappointed at the fact she can't try to offer them my hand in marriage. I walk them through everything from the unanswered calls to the front door. I scroll through her medical profile on our insurance app and try to give them all of the information on her stage of dementia and symptoms she'd been having while they both take notes in those little memo pads they all seem to carry. I try my best not to cry since I remember Mom telling me how it makes me look weak and overly dramatic, but I'm scared shitless. After a while of what I'm sure they considered overexplaining, they tell me the first step is to have all on duty officers patrol the immediate area to see if they can locate her. I give them a recent photo to use if they need it and they inform me that the optimal result is quickly finding her close to home, but without knowing how long she's been gone and how long she's been out in the desert heat, it's a race against time and the elements.

Giving both officers my contact information, I watch them drive slowly down the road as the darkness settles in. Wanting to drive around by myself since I can't just sit around and wait, I knock on the neighbor's door to let her know what's going on in case Mom comes back while I'm gone. Kathy, divorced and in her mid-50s, has always been kind to us, even after a few instances Mom called her every name under the sun when she thought Kathy was stealing our mail. She does her best to control her panic around me to keep things optimistic, and gladly agrees to keep an eye out.

While the police are already on the search, I don't waste any time jumping in my car to drive the grid I'm envisioning in my mind. She can't be too far.

# CHAPTER TWO

## Clif

I might stare up at the game on the tv behind the bar, but really, I don't give a shit about basketball. I don't give a shit about much of anything anymore, and the things I do give a shit about revolve around cards, cash, and my little brother, Joseph. He should be sitting here next to me right now with his own Jack and Coke, but instead, he's stuck in a cell in gen pop and it's all my fucking fault.

I don't know how things got so screwed up so fast, but it's all a blur when I try to think back to where exactly I lost control of everything and everyone in my life. One second I'm playing the best couple hands of hold 'em I've ever played, and then the next I'm down more money than I've ever had and Walter, the owner of Marrin's Pub, has my back against the wall giving me a week to repay with interest. When they threw me out, Joseph picked me up and I came clean about what the fuck just happened, and how deep into trouble I'd gotten without realizing it. I hated telling him. He's the younger one, so I always called him Little Joey – even now. He's supposed to be the irresponsible brother, but I was always the mess. Joey is the only living member of the Wallace family to be proud of for anything. Kid's a fucking genius.

For five days, we tried to sell anything we could get our hands on from pills to pot, but we weren't getting close enough to the stack of high society I owed. If you incessantly watched the movie "Rounders" like I did when I was a kid, you'd know already that means I owe Walter $10,000 plus interest. The night before the debt was due, we sat in our apartment and decided on the dumbest fucking idea we could have ever had. We'd find a place or two to hold up, preferably with no customers or cameras, and a clerk about 100 years old.

Driving around with fucking balaclavas in our hoodie pockets and the gun dad left behind when he died, we picked the two spots we knew we'd have the best chance of hitting without getting busted. Our only hope was that we'd get enough cash off those two joints to make it to the drop in the morning and then that was it - no more fucking cards. It had to be enough money because I didn't have a plan if it wasn't. Little Joey drove my car since I didn't want him holding a gun in case shit went south. Not only is he a shit shot, but he shakes when he gets anxious, and I can't have him in a position where someone could get the jump on him.

We rolled into the parking lot of the first spot, a liquor store called Mirage that was owned by a senior couple that liked to keep the business old school. Most of the tourists and spring breakers prefer to hit up the bigger, more Instagrammable locations closer to the downtown areas and hotels, so we found Mirage and A-1's. Both spots were a little off the beaten path and the clientele was older and less likely to pass a background check or a DUI checkpoint.

Covering our faces, Joey stayed in the car while I rushed into Mirage right up to the old woman behind the counter. She didn't even put up a fight, just opened the register and the safe to hand me whatever she had. I know she must have hit an alert button, but aside from that, I was in and out without anyone making a scene or getting hurt. As we rushed away and pulled the covers from our faces, we sped to A-1 so we could get in while the police were en route to Mirage. It seemed like the perfect plan when we talked about it over beers and blunts the night before.

Turns out, it wasn't the perfect plan. When I went to do the same routine as the last place, I wasn't expecting this one to have an off-duty cop picking up his dirty habit. I was barely out the door before I heard the sirens and not long after that, we saw the blue and red lights. We thought maybe we should just dump the damn car somewhere and go pick it up later, but when Joey pulled over, the lights and sirens turned out to be closer than we thought. He told me we were going to jump and run. Hell, it was dark as fuck out there, it would have been fine. But my little brother was always looking out for me, so when I jumped out of the car with the backpack of money, the gun, and our balaclavas, he shut the door and drove off with the cops not too far off his ass. He got 26 years and I barely got $3,500. That was three weeks ago today.

I gave Walter two grand out of that money, and I've been avoiding that slimy mother fucker since. Every once in a while, he'll send his lackeys and I'll bide myself a little time, but all I need is the rest of Walter's money and enough for a lawyer to file an appeal. Joey's free lawyer was a damn moron, and there was never enough evidence to charge him with armed robbery, but somehow, it was enough to sentence him. We both know it wasn't right, but like everything else in this fucked up world, it costs money to fix it. Money got him in, and I need money to get him out. While he's in there, I'm out here trying to find tables I can sit in on to play or anything else I can do for money. Time is ticking for me and for my brother, and I feel like there's no way for us to get out of this safely. He was supposed to be the one that made something of himself between the both of us, and his only weakness was a good heart.

Tired of staring at the stupid game on tv, I nod to Charlene behind the bar to load me up with another Jack and Coke when I come back. For now, I'm itching for a smoke and I'm pissed off you can't light up inside anymore. Heading out the back past the bathrooms, I prop the door with the small rock next to the coffee can everyone throws their butts in. When the warm night air hits me, I put the filter between my lips and light a match from the book I grabbed from the bartop. Through a deep inhale, I unzip my fly and kill two birds with one stone as I relieve myself on the wall.

When I hear footsteps, I quickly tuck back into my black jeans and zip up, not trying to meet whoever is walking down a dark alley with my dick out. I don't get the chance to focus my eyes on either man before one of them shoves their fist right into my face. I try to return the fucking favor, but the other one delivers a punch right to my gut, making me thankful I emptied my bladder or I would have just pissed myself. I put my hands up to protect my face at least, but before I know it, I'm thrown down the four uneven stairs onto the asphalt.

I don't need a mirror to tell me I'm bleeding. I can taste the shitty tinge of copper in my mouth and it makes me want to gag. It's fucking gross, but I get to my feet as best I can, hating myself for making that first Jack and Coke a double. Maybe then I could have blocked the next hit that landed right under my chin to knock me back on the ground, or the several kicks to my back and abdomen right after.

When I stop moving as much to just accept whatever this is, the men stop assaulting my tired frame and start digging through my pockets. I'm a little fuzzy, but fuck, if they wanted to jack my wallet, they didn't have to do all this shit. I blink through the blur of my watering eyes, and I can hear my keys. Not my goddamn car. Fuck.

"Aye, can you hear us, Clif?" the taller one asks while he shakes my keys like you would to entertain a fussy infant. I groan.

"You ain't paid Walter, and we're here to take some collateral and deliver a message. You can negotiate your car back when you pay up. You get a week," the short, round man in an out of date fedora says.

I spit the bloody saliva in my mouth onto the black top and try to stand. "Thanks. Y-you could have just sent a text, dicks."

"Now, now. Don't be impolite, Clifton. That's not the full message. We're here to tell you that if you don't pay your debts, we'll collect it in your brother's blood," the taller one threatens with a teasing voice that makes me want to rage. "We got all kinds of ways to reach him in there. Don't forget that when you're fuckin' around instead of getting Walter's money."

I make it to my feet with a slight sway to show as much strength as I can, or at least some god damned dignity. "How am I supposed t-to get his cash without a fucking car?"

"Should have thought of that before you started livin' above your means, man," the round one taunts.

"Yeah, not our problem, is it?" the tall one laughs. They both turn to walk away clicking the lock button on the fob to make the black BMW's lights flash. "Seven days, Clifton, or your brother is on the other end of another inmate altercation."

I watch them walk away, and then I hear the car fire up and peel out of the other side of the alley. I stand there for a minute letting everything settle in and without meaning to, I disassociate. When I snap into troubleshooting mode, I pat my bruised body to take inventory of what they left me with since now I have no fucking car.

FUCK. I need a car. What the fuck am I supposed to do without a car? Uber to a robbery?

In my front right pocket, I have one poker chip that I always hold to get me out of trouble if I need quick cash. In my back pocket, I have exactly $24 which I was planning on using to pay Charlene for my drinks, but now I can't. And then in my front left pocket, I have a pearl-handled switchblade. They definitely would have jacked my knife if I hadn't been almost unconscious on top of it. A poker chip, $24, and a switchblade. How can I MacGyver that shit into the $8,000 I still owe Walter plus interest on top of whatever else I need to get back my car?

# CHAPTER THREE

## Sonnet, Three Years Ago

*M*y mother and I sit in the car silently on the way back to her house. We'd just left the third doctor's appointment, and as much as she made my childhood hell, I can't help but feel the mixed emotions she must have after the hopeful expectation of this one telling her something she wanted to hear. Instead, we're both quiet. The radio is off and every time I glance over at her, she's just staring blankly out the window. Her eyes aren't even moving as the cars and desert mountain range drift by. It's like her body and soul have reached an overload point and she's just frozen in a state of buffering.

As I pass by McDonald's, I offer to swing through the drive thru for a Diet Coke and some fries, but she subtly shakes her head. I've been angry at this woman for decades, but all of it dissipates in seeing her try to process what the grim future of dementia holds for her. Even the best case scenario could make anyone lose hope when the good and bad news are all wrapped around the speed of its progression. Good days will come less and less as time goes on, and they'll usually just mean the absence of a *bad day. Someone should call them "plateau" days instead if they're just a day you escape a noticeable decline.*

*My mind coasts through the possibilities, and what she's going to do now that a treatment plan will need to be in place. I know there's no way to shield her from the conversations we'll have to have at this point. No one wants to hear the words "nursing home", but when you're living alone with dementia, there's going to come a time of inevitability. We may not be there yet, but there's no exact science to each individual's personal timeline. With me working at the hospital, I'm able to swap shifts around to check on her more, but it's not going to be a permanent solution like a nursing home would.*

*When I pull up the driveway and into the garage, no one rushes to get out of the car when I turn it off. Before I even plan out what to say, I blurt the first thing I know Dad would have wanted.*

*"Mom, let me move back home. My lease is up in a month and I can just stay with you to help out," I offer nervously. I don't want to get into another fight with her, but her pride is what's made this diagnosis so delayed. She shoots a glare at me and narrows her eyes, and I regret voicing the suggestion instantly even if I know it was the right thing to do.*

*"Oh, fuck off, Sonnet. I don't need a nurse," she snaps and I wince. She fidgets with her seatbelt, her fingers giving her trouble with the red release button. Her frustration is loud and clear through her huffs and puffs. As much as her words bite like usual, I understand these ones aren't resentful, they're painful.*

*"Not as a nurse, Mom, as your daughter," I clarify and she pauses her movements to look up at me. Her eyes no longer hold the fierce fire that wants to curse the world for the chip she carries on her shoulder. She's looking at me like a regular woman who's just received life changing*

news, and not for the better. I see that look in faces at the hospital all the time, but it looks so different when it's worn by my own mother.

She opens her mouth to speak and closes it. Without another word, I reach over to click the button to release her seatbelt. I can see the relief on her face that she didn't have to continue her struggle or ask me for help with a task that used to be simple. She pulls her designer purse from the floor, swinging it over her shoulder and walking proudly to the door that leads to the kitchen. Before she reaches it, she turns back and when I open my car door, she puts a hand out to stop me.

"I appreciate the ride. I'll call you if I need anything," she says in a cold, informal tone like she's trying to separate me from this personal part of her life. As if I didn't drive her there and sit with her myself for every single appointment since she's no longer driving the Mustang parked in the space next to me.

Swallowing down my feelings, I remind myself this is detachment and she just needs time. Before I get the chance to say anything back, she turns and she walks into the house, giving me a quick glimpse into the kitchen for a moment until I'm in the garage surrounded by silence. I close my car door, feeling the pangs of hunger twist my stomach, and I back out of the driveway. When I reach the road to put the car in drive, I see the curtains shift slightly where the living room is, and I know she's watching even if I can't see her. Pushing the button, the garage door closes.

Driving back to my apartment, I stop by my favorite sushi spot for dragon rolls, grilled salmon rolls with eel sauce, and of course, the best damn gyoza in the whole state. I don't actually have the data to back that up, but I would believe it if someone said it. With a brown paper takeout bag under my arm, I can't open the door to my apartment fast enough. I'm practically drooling at the smell of my "treat yourself" dinner.

I don't even change out of my clothes, I just peel off everything except my lacy boy shorts and then throw on a t-shirt before sitting on my couch and arranging my mini-buffet on the coffee table. Wrapped in two different blankets, I flip through the new options on every streaming service I subscribe to while I inhale more sushi than any human should in one sitting. I could cry at how wonderful it tastes combined with the sheer exhaustion from today, and I almost do. Had it not been for the "Are Mermaids Real?" documentary I settled into, I might have let my mind pull my heart into a depressing spiral.

After several hours, I'm still scrolling through book recommendations and adding them to my wish lists online when my phone vibrates in my hand, scaring the shit out of me. It's almost 11pm and I don't recognize the phone number. It's not entirely uncommon for the hospital to give my number to the new staff, especially on the night shifts, so I quickly swipe to answer mentally hoping they're not going to tell me they need me to come in for a double again.

"Hi, I'm sorry, but is this Sonnet Franklin?" The voice is female and possibly older, but I don't immediately feel a connection or know who she is. Her tone sounds nervous, but it's not likely a spammer at this hour.

"Speaking," I answer cautiously, not wanting to give anything away just in case. I almost hear a sigh of relief before she lowers her tone like she's going to share a secret, but people are closeby.

"Sweetie, I'm sorry to disturb you. I'm Kathy, your momma's neighbor, and I have her over at my house right now. She calmed down a lot, but she came over here claiming I stole her mail or tried to break into her house," she whispers and I can hear my mother's agitated voice in the background. I can't make out what she's saying, but it doesn't matter. This is one of the reasons we even started talking to doctors in the first place. After a few instances of frustrated confusion and motor issues, I started to suspect the decline.

*"Oh my god, I'm so sorry. Ok, I'll come over. I'm sorry. Thank you," I stumble through my words while I throw my warm blanket burrito situation to the other end of the couch and start looking for my sweatpants.*

*"It's alright, dear. My grandma had Alzheimer's too. It's a tough ride, hon. We'll be here and I'll put the porch light on. Just come right in," she says with a tone that offered the support and comfort I'd never even heard from my own mom.*

*I mumble my way through a goodbye and pack a few things in my bag to make sure I can spend the night and head right into my shift tomorrow. I don't know how many nights I'll have to stay with her, but I can at least get through tonight, and then we'll have to learn to trust each other and take it one day at a time. As I sling my backpack over my shoulder and flip the switch for the living room lights, I have a moment of silence in my cozy one bedroom place.*

*My apartment has been such a source of sanctuary for me, a peaceful little paradise I carved out for myself that my mother and her ire had never stepped foot into. Even though it wasn't the nuclear family with a white picket fenced house my mother insisted was the right way to spend my life, it was completely mine and I loved it. Looking from my bookshelves to my thrift store sourced furniture and decor, it was everything that made me feel warm and the most like myself.*

*With one heavy sigh, I closed the door behind me and locked it knowing it would be one of the last times I'd go through this motion. With the developments of Mom's disease, and her inevitable refusal to voluntarily live in a nursing home, I knew she'd decide to take me up on the impulsive offer to move back into my old room downstairs. Back to the place where I cried myself to sleep every night to dream of a realm where none of this existed and I was a Dragon Princess that knew how to fight back.*

# CHAPTER FOUR

## Sonnet

The world got darker as the precious seconds to find Mom turned into minutes and then to an hour. My tension headache began to sting behind my eyes as I squinted to look closer at the driver and passenger in each car I passed, the people walking through parking lots, and the tables against the windows of the local restaurants. For a moment, I see her in every one of their faces, but then I blink and she's gone and I'm still searching.

As I approach the second hour, I stop into my fifth business, a grocery store, and show them the photo I have of her on my phone. I ask the young girl with pink braids if she's seen my mother and she shakes her head with a sympathetic expression. I wonder how many people I've stopped have experienced a loved one going through dementia. Based on the way some of them looked at the picture, then to me with softened eyes, I'm guessing three. With another failed attempt on the list in my head, I pull back onto the road to make my way to the next place.

Trying to blink away the heaviness weighing down my eyelids, I'm still exhausted from the day I've had and the long night that preceded it. Mom had what her doctor's would refer to as a bad day, and when day turned to night, she was the cruelest she'd ever been. I tried to tell myself that it was the disease making her say and do those things, but the undertone of her torment had existed long before her diagnosis. Most days I felt alone in knowing who my mother really was, since like a true beauty queen, she knew when she was on stage and when she wasn't. Aside from protecting her delicate image, she stole my ability to find camaraderie with anyone else in my position. I'd tried attending the support group the doctor recommended for family caregivers, but when I sat down to listen, I felt even more isolated. Sometimes I forget that not everyone has a strained tumultuous relationship with their immediate family, and now at 38, she's the only part of it I have left.

Getting back into my car after another failed attempt, this time at Mom's favorite ice cream shop, I crank up the AC and call Kathy to update her. With Kathy's solemn tone, she reports that there's no news back home, so she's alerted her friends from the local library's book club. Thanking her for her diligence and kindness, I call the officers back who gave me their card to hear they aren't any father in finding her either. They tell me the next step is for them to issue a silver alert due to the length of time away from the residence, her not having a phone, and the temperature outside. I feel like I've said thank you too much and not enough as I hang up and think about the next places I'll check while I widen my search grid.

Turning right down Pollock Circle, I notice that the small light next to the gas tank icon is blaring bright against my dark dash to let me know that I'm officially past the point of acceptable procrastination. Almost at the same time, my stomach aches with hunger and I realize I haven't had much to eat or drink since my stop at McDonald's on the way home. I contemplate not stopping, but something from the support group echoes in my tired mind. *You can't help others if you don't also help yourself.* Sighing with acceptance, I decide to stop at the next gas station that I haven't already been to so I can fill the tank, grab some snacks, and ask the cashier if they've seen my mother.

A few miles later, I'm lining up to pump 3 at a BP gas station on a long stretch of road bordering the desert. It's the only light source for a while, and it doesn't look like there's anything down that way aside from the ramp to the interstate. It's not in an incredibly busy part of town aside from a dive bar, a liquor store, and of course a couple churches to balance it out. I don't think my mother would have made it this far, but I can't rule anything out at this point. *Maybe someone gave her a ride.* When the handle clicks to alert me that the tank is full, I head inside with my phone to follow my routine. I peruse the aisles not knowing what I'm interested in since there's so much going on in my head that I'm hungry for all of it and none of it at the same time.

I grab a peanut butter granola bar, a Slim Jim that looks like it's almost 2 feet long, a box of rainbow Nerds, and a big bottle of water to hold me over until I call off the search at the end of the night with hopefully good news. It wasn't a balanced meal by any means, but any time spent parked in my car eating a McDinner is time I'm not spending looking for my mother. As a cashier with a name tag that says "Hi, I'm Dennis! Ask me about our BP credit card!" puts my items in a white plastic bag, I show him the picture of Mom on my phone. He tells me she's beautiful and he can see where I get my looks, but gives me the same sympathetic eyes as three other people today. I try not to feel defeated as I thank him for looking before I sulk back outside.

"I'll keep an eye out for your ma, sweetheart," he calls on my way out the door, but I don't turn back.

When I get to the car, I throw the bag of snacks on the passenger side, and mindlessly flop into my seat trying to find the energy to keep up the search. Of course I want to find her, but I'm so tired. The only thing that keeps me going is the guilt I know I'll feel if I stop. After taking a deep breath, I turn the key and start pulling out onto the desert road. Feeling my stomach rumble louder, I keep my left hand on the wheel as I use my right to reach for the plastic bag on the seat next to me. I only pat my hand on the cushion twice before I suddenly feel a firm grip wrapped around my wrist. With a gasp, I try to turn my head on impulse, but at the same time, a large figure sits up in my backseat and pushes what feels like a knife into my side. With the inability to move my right arm, my left is firmly gripped around the steering wheel and I freeze as I watch the rearview mirror slowly fill with his frame as he sits up.

As dark as it is, I can make out his medium length black hair and what looks to be a sharp set of blue eyes that could cut me down for his own amusement. I want to scream. I want to run the car off of the road. I want to suddenly know martial arts. But I do nothing. I freeze.

"Just drive," his low voice instructs as he pushes the knife a little deeper into the space between my ribs. If he was going to stab me, he could have done it already, so that means he wants something else from me. I almost gag as I start to think about everything he could take from me, and the panic sets in faster than I was ready for. My breathing turns shallow and rapid while my skin feels like I'm being poked with needles all over my body in waves. I know what a panic attack feels like, but there's no way I can calm myself down now. Shit. *Please don't pass out again.*

"You don't understand. The police-" I start, but he cuts me off with a nonchalant expression on his face and a scoff.

"Nope, no cops. We're doing this my way. You drive, get us on the interstate, and I'll tell you when to pull off," he says, his voice dripping in a threatening air of authority. Out of instinct, I try to jerk my wrist out of his hold anyway. His knife leaves my side instantly as he uses his hand to grab a handful of my hair and jerk my head back forcefully, burning my scalp. "You fucking try anything, and I mean *anything*, and I'll throw you in the fucking trunk. You get me?"

Tears forming, I nod my head as much as I can while he has my hair in a vice grip, and I feel the fear start to consume me. "Please, no trunk. I'm claustrophobic, please. I-I-I can't. I can't. Don't lock me in the trunk. I'll die in there."

"Then be a good girl and don't make me do it. Understand?" he asks, squeezing my hair just a little harder. I can feel the sting at the roots, bringing my tension headache to the back of my skull. I try to nod in compliance so he knows I'll cooperate, but I can't move in his grip. All I can do to not crash my car is keep my eyes lowered to see the road while he's got my head tilted back to expose my neck like I'm preparing for slaughter.

"Y-yes. O-k. Ok," I stutter out and he releases my hair with a shove that pushes my upper half forward. I keep my body rigid in place while I drive carefully so I can think of how to safely get myself out of this, but my mind is racing with thoughts of my missing mother, self defense lessons, and worst case scenarios I've seen on every true crime documentary.

*What happens if they locate my mother, but I'm dead? Who will take care of her?*

*What does he want from me that he needs to take me out to the middle of the desert?*

*Where are we going?*

*Am I going to survive him? This?*

*If I make it through this alive, will it destroy me?*

*Can I flag down a cop?*

*Is my phone close enough to me?*

*If I wreck this car while wearing a seatbelt like in the movies, what are the chances that I can make it?*

*What happens when we get to where he's taking me?*

*Mom, I'm so sorry. I'm sorry I wasn't who you wanted me to be. Forgive me.*

# CHAPTER FIVE

## Clif

Holding a hand to my bruised side, I stand up straight to stretch my body, assessing how fucked I actually am. It stings, but I'm not puking or pissing blood yet so that has to be a good sign. I can't go back inside because now I can't pay for my drinks, but I don't know where the hell I'm supposed to go without a car, so I just start walking. Not realizing it was past 11pm, I try to think if I know anyone I can crash with in walking distance, but I come up with fuck all. I can't even get back to my place to change my clothes. Shit.

After less than ten minutes of walking and feeling sorry for myself, I find a BP gas station and I squint to see who's behind the counter. If it's Trent, that would give me at least one person that gave a shit about Joey and might hook me up with a ride home. Hell, I'd take a free pack of smokes and a hot dog too if he's offering. As I get closer, the inside comes into view and it's some guy I've never seen at the counter, so there goes that plan. Coming up to the side of the building, I lean to rest but stay out of sight since I'm sure I look like I feel. Last thing I need is the fucking cops called on me.

I'm only there for a few minutes before I see one car pull in and a redhead get out. She's short, wearing blue scrubs, and not paying any attention as she fills up her tank. At first, I consider just approaching her to ask for money, but when I think about what I must look like, I realize there's no way she won't call for help. I know my face is banged up, but between my tattoos and the weight of the world on my shoulders, I'm lucky I'm in all black or she'd see the blood too. I don't want her to scream or call the cops, shit, nowadays every chick carries a couple weapons like mace or tasers and I can't afford to be in any worse of a spot than I am now.

I watch her for a little bit, trying to decide the best way to get what I need from her since she's probably going to be the only car for who knows how long. When her tank is full, she walks inside, still staring down at her phone and mumbling to herself. I know my window of opportunity is shrinking, and I do the only thing I can think of. Looking into the store and seeing her distracted, I jog over to her car and check the handle. Unlocked. I impulsively slip into the back seat and lie low, counting on the darkness of the night and the station's shitty lighting to hide me until we're on the road long enough for me to take her car. If I take her car and leave her in the desert with no phone, that buys me a good amount of time to do whatever I need to do. Maybe she's wearing a fancy wedding ring or some shit and it's worth a couple grand. Too bad her car isn't worth anything at a chop shop. I'll just wing this shit. I don't have another option. Joey's counting on me.

I hold my breath steady as she opens her door, throwing a bag on the passenger seat before she hops in to start the car. When she buckles her seatbelt, I get a whiff of her floral shampoo and I can't help but inhale. Maybe it's because I haven't gotten laid in a long time by anyone I gave a shit about. Sure there were girls here and there, but it was never serious because I'm a selfish asshole with no desire to be locked down. I almost let pussy come between me and Joey once, but now that I got my head on straight, I'm done with chicks like Willa. Now, I'd rather be married to the game since that's all that's ever made me feel anything. Winning a big pot has brought me more happiness than any woman anyway.

Snapping back into reality, I grit my teeth and ready myself to move when she pulls out of the parking lot. I can feel the roughness of the road under her tires and after about two minutes, she reaches over to the passenger seat for her bag. Grabbing her wrist, I sit up slowly and hold my pearl-handled knife to her side just enough for her to know I'm not fucking around. I don't plan on ever having to use it, but I have to scare her. I can't afford for her to fight back right now because in the state I'm in, she might be able to get the jump on me. The element of surprise is my biggest asset.

I can feel her freeze and white-knuckle the steering wheel with her left hand, but when she looks at me in the rear view mirror, I'm relieved when her expression tells me she knows I'm in control. Even with her nonverbal admission, her body fidgets, unable to let her survival instincts accept the futility of the fight yet. I tell her to drive and Little Red tries to jerk her wrist out of my hold like someone who hasn't fully realized how much bigger I am than she is. I can appreciate the cute effort though, so I try not to scare her too much, but I need her to do exactly as I say. I really don't want to hurt her, but I need her to think I might so I can secure her compliance and get this shit over with as quickly as possible.

"You don't understand. The police-" she starts to tell me, but I have to make sure she knows that I don't give a fuck about the cops. The only thing that genuinely scares me is that she'll make me do something that'll land me in the pen for life or worse. And I can't help Joey if I'm dead or gone. I glare at her.

"Nope, no cops. We're doing this my way. You drive, get us on the interstate, and I'll tell you when to pull off," I tell her. When I feel her pull her right arm as hard as she can to free herself from my grasp, I do what I fucking have to do. I squeeze her small wrist tighter and use the other to grab a chunk of her hair from the back, holding my knife in my grip with it so I never let it leave my hand. I pull her hair back toward me exposing her neck, forcing her to strain her eyes to see the road.

"You fucking try anything, and I mean anything, and I'll throw you in the fucking trunk. You get me?"

For some reason when I mention the trunk she freaks the fuck out and starts to panic. I'm sure every self defense and true crime show tells these women never let men like me get you in the trunk, so I hope I can use that to my advantage because the way she's breathing tells me that scares her more than my knife does. The more terrified she is, the faster I can get her to do this shit and I can be done with it.

"Then be a good girl and don't make me do it. Understand?" I ask her, and I pull her hair again partly to make sure she knows I'm not fucking around, and partly because I kinda like the sound she makes when I do. *I know. I got problems.*

She says she understands and we keep driving. The farther we go, the more her eyes move and I can tell she's trying to figure out where we're going and why. Her eyes are shifting around like she's trying to mentally log everything from my full description to where we're going. When the sign for I-445 pops up, I press the knife back into her side causing her to sharply inhale.

"Take the exit," I tell her and without even thinking, she flips on her turn signal.

Before we can merge, her phone starts blaring a noise I've heard before when some big warning is issued. We both look at it and she fidgets like she's itching to read it. I can see it light up from the passenger seat and before she can think, I release her wrist and grab her phone. When I look at the screen it's a silver alert issued with a photo. An elderly person with dementia is missing in the area and is in danger. Hearing her sniffle and grip the wheel with both hands, I start to piece everything together. The distracted look, the tired expression, the growl of her stomach, and the mention of police. She wasn't talking about me, she must be involved in this somehow. Fucking great. This was supposed to be simple.

"Who is this to you?" I ask her as we ride down the interstate going nowhere. I pause the idea of finding a desert spot to dump her while I get her to answer the question. When she doesn't reply immediately, I press my knife in and a tear rolls down her face.

"That's my mom. She has dementia and she wandered from the house when I was at work. We can't find her and I don't know how long she's been out here in the heat alone and confused," she sniffles. "P-please just let me go. I need to find her."

As much as I've had to harden my heart to keep myself from being weak, I regret getting in this car tonight, but we're too far to stop now. It's too late. I need the car, money, and anything else I can take from her to help me get out of this mess I'm in. She pleads with me through her eyes in the rearview mirror, but I keep my expression emotionless so she knows there's no chance I'll be persuaded. If it's between her mom and my brother, I gotta choose Joey.

Before I can tell her to stop crying, I see a cop car coming up fast behind us in the lane to our left. I don't even have to guess what she's thinking because as soon as he starts to pass, she tries to make eye contact and swerve. I reach up and grab the wheel to steady it, and as if by some lucky cosmic coincidence, he flips on his sirens to chase a speeding sports car far ahead of us. She screams in frustration and starts thrashing, and I keep a hand on the wheel as I climb up to the front seat to hold the knife at her throat.

Her eyes go wide at the size difference in the two of us and I push her to take the next exit since apparently we need to have a talk about following the fucking directions so no one gets hurt. She tries to plead, but it's too damn late. That was a close call and I can't do this shit with her all night. She won't survive it and I'll be even farther from paying Walter and getting Joey out of jail.

When we drive down the side road we took the exit for, it's almost midnight and out here there's barely any lighting or civilization. I'm glad it's mostly deserted because I can't have witnesses see me stuff her bratty ass in the trunk so I can think...and probably eat her snacks from the station. I'm fucking hungry too now. The moment I throw it in park, she starts screaming at the top of her lungs and without thinking, I grab the back of her head and throw her face into the steering wheel. I thought it would just scare her so she knows I'm serious, but when I bring her back up, she's got a gash on her head and there's blood dripping down her face and into her mouth. Shit. Shit. Shiiiiiiiiiiit.

She's a little disoriented, so I take those few seconds to pull the keys out of the ignition and run around the front and to her side. She doesn't even get the chance to fight me as I pull her out of the car and pop the trunk from the button on the dash. As she starts becoming more alert, the fear sobers her instantly when she realizes what I have to do. I warned her. Pulling and fighting me with strength I'm surprised she has, I drag her by her hair toward the back of the car where the trunk is slightly ajar.

With the volume of the scuffle, I put my sore muscles into it and yank her body weight into mine. When we reach the back of the car, she reacts like I'm about to throw her into a vat of acid but there's nothing I can do. I really fucking warned her. Pressing her back to my front, I hold her around the waist with one arm to lift her off the ground and prevent her from kicking me. I use my other hand to lift the trunk. When the interior light goes on, I drop her on the ground and freeze.

Only she's not screaming anymore...she's...laughing. I stare into the trunk at the old woman with a face twisted in terror, and all I can hear is Little Red's insane cackling. As she stands, I look at her and the image scares the piss out of me. The blood that dripped into the cracks between her teeth glows in the dim interior light from the trunk.

"I forgot about that," she shrugs and laughs. "I knew I forgot something."

I turn and prepare myself to empty the contents of my stomach, but nothing comes out. I don't have anything in my system but the remnants of my double Jack and Coke and the increasing fear of what the fuck I just got myself into with this Little Killer.

# Chapter Six

## Sonnet, Last Night

*No one tells you how hard it is to grow up with a difficult parent and then be the only one left to care for them when they get older. My mother has resented me since the day I was born and she's always reminded me of what having me cost her. A crown. A sash. A lifelong career and future in the Miss America lifestyle. When it wasn't part of her lifeplan anymore, she made peace with that by assuming that she could pass it down to me and I'd happily live her dreams for her. She could be the pageant mom instead of the pageant queen, so at least half of her would still be on that stage doing a practiced wave. If it hadn't been for Dad telling me I could do whatever activities I wanted and letting me steer clear of it, I probably would have been one of those little toddler beauty queens on reality tv.*

*She was always this bad, but she hid it so well in front of Dad. When he passed over ten years ago, she didn't have to hide her resentment anymore because the one person she cared about was gone. The heart attack was a shock to us both, but Mom felt like I didn't deserve to be as sad as she was since it was my fault somehow. My fault I didn't die instead.*

*When I got home from working a 14 hour shift, every part of my body was screaming to rest. Mom was fine for the day, and I made sure I called and checked in constantly since I try not to leave her alone for more than 5 hours or so. Even then, I text Kathy to go over for some made up reason so I can have her do a wellness check. It's not a sustainable system, but for now it works. There isn't much longer we can keep this up before a change will have to be made. A few coworkers have told me about great nursing homes and other assisted living facilities for people that are going through the same stage of dementia as Mom, and it would be nice for her to have other people to do things with.*

*When I walked inside the house, she had a mess in the kitchen and she was humming to herself. I cursed in my head and tried to go over the reminders to myself that it's a cruel disease that makes you act like someone else at times. I stepped further into the kitchen to see everything that was happening as she zipped around from stove top to microwave to the table where she'd set two plates for us. My heart warmed a little at the effort she was making to show me she cared, and I thought maybe this was her way of saying things she couldn't find the words to express. She loved me. She was proud of me. She was happy to be a family.*

*Warmly hugging me as I made my presence known, she smiled and motioned for me to take a seat. I was caught off guard, but wanted to take the opportunity to enjoy every second of her being the mother I always wanted since there was no way of knowing how long it would last. When I sat at the table, she pushed in my chair and kissed the top of my head. I almost let a tear slip as the love-starved kid in my soul felt the whisper of what my childhood could have been. Where had this part of my mother been locked up and what happened today to turn the key? Whatever it was, I was grateful that I could have this gift even if it never came again.*

*Putting a plate of messy spaghetti heavily sprinkled with parmesan cheese in front of me, she gave me a glass of water and sat next to me while she excitedly watched. It was like a chef waiting for someone to try their newest addition to the menu.*

*"Where's yours, Mom?" I asked her since I thought if she was making dinner we'd at least pretend to have a nice family meal with just the two of us. She just smiled at me and motioned for me to eat, even though her plate remained empty.*

*"I don't need anything, dear. This is just for you," she said sweetly, looking at me with doting eyes. "I should have done better by you..." she trailed off as she watched me twirl my fork on the plate to wrap around noodles.*

*I lifted the utensil to my mouth, but the millisecond before it reached my lips, I smelled something off. I drew my brows together, and pulled my fork back to look at the noodles with the powdered cheese, but that's not what I noticed. As my eyes blurred the food in front of my mouth, my mother's face came into focus and a sensation of pure, unadulterated dread washed through me. She was looking at me with an anxiously sinister expression, like something terrible was about to happen at any moment. Spooked, I dropped the fork on my plate and she began to twist her features into a sneer.*

*"I made this special for you and you better finish every single bite, Sonnet Elizabeth Franklin. I mean it. I said so. You have to," she demanded, but instead of coming off with maternal authority, she sounded desperate. Like she needed me to eat it. Whatever was going on, I was done with it.*

*I slid my chair back and stood from the table. Faster than she expected, I grabbed my plate to scrape the contents into the trash. The moment she saw me lift the lid to the trash can, she flew up from her chair to try to pull me back, but it was too late. My skin crawled with what I saw. Laying on* top of the other contents of the trash, there was an empty jar of marinara sauce and an empty box from the pasta, but next to it there was another box. After a quick look at the picture, I knew what it was even if shock had set in and I didn't want to believe it. Rat poison. Fucking. Rat. Poison.

"Eat your food," she yelled at me as she tried to salvage the fork still rolled with a bit of spaghetti on it. She lunged to wrestle it into my mouth, but I pulled my lips in between my teeth to clamp my jaw shut.

I wanted to tell her to stop, but I was scared to open my mouth in fear she'd find a way to get that powder into my body for good. Pulling back as she grabbed out for my hair or anything to latch onto, I heard her grumble her clear intentions under her breath.

"Waste...little waste...worthless...taken from me," she grunted out and I knew what I'd always known my entire life. Her love was conditionally based upon my participation, my compliance, and my ability to finish what she started before she got pressured into living the life she clearly resented. I shoved her backward and she narrowed her eyes in sheer hatred.

"No husband. No children. You have nothing. I have nothing to show for everything I sacrificed for you. I should have never had you. One trip to the clinic and I would have been somebody!"

The words stung even though I'd heard them over and over throughout my life as soon as Dad died. Without him to stop her, she retired the passive aggressive and resorted straight to aggressive aggressive. I'd always known she didn't love me, but this was so far past fucked up. As soon as she uttered the words, she ran at me with her arms out. Maybe it was to push me into the garage door or strangle me, I had no idea, but I braced myself for the impact as I yelled at her to stop.

She cried at me, trying to grasp for my neck, but I reached behind me to turn the knob of the garage door. When it gave, we tumbled in next to my car and when she took a moment to look at her beloved Mustang, I grabbed her. I wrapped my arms around her tightly and wrangled her as I reached into my pocket for my keys. I was going to take her to the ER and let them handle her crazy ass or maybe to the police station, but when I pushed the buttons blindly the doors locked and the trunk popped open.

She turned in my hold to reach for my neck and I tried to get around the car to put distance between us, but when I was scared I might not win, I pushed her. She stumbled back a step against the open trunk, and without another thought, I shoved her in and threw the top down.

I ran back into the kitchen and shut the door, leaning against it while I breathed heavily and felt my heart pound through my chest. Mom? Mommy? My brain raced and I tried to blink away what just happened and make sense of the reality. With control slipping, I got a handle on what I could manage. Baby steps. I cleaned up the mess from dinner, wiped down the countertops, and took the tainted meal out to the large trash bin against the side of the house.

With it being garbage day in the morning, I walked it to the curb and considered myself lucky to be alive. I didn't know what I'd do next, but what I did know is that I couldn't handle her while she was awake. If I admitted what she did, she'd be locked away. I'd have to let her tucker herself out and then I could call someone to come get her. There wasn't any other choice. Maybe this would finally be the breaking point to have her in a home, or hospitalized, because this is past the city limits of unhinged. This can't be real life. This can't be real. It isn't real. I kept saying it to myself while my eyes blurred. Tired.

Laying on the couch, I decided to give her an hour to see if it would be enough time for her to pass out. Mom? Pretend everything is ok. Everything is ok. Just a normal night. I stretched out and scrolled on my phone, watching the time go by until I closed my eyes.

*I shook myself awake with the light streaming in through the living room windows and I looked down at my scrubs. Unable to recall why I didn't change when I got home, I wrote it off to another wild full moon night at work, and walked to the bathroom to take a shower. I didn't see Mom anywhere so I figured she was probably still asleep. I contemplated checking on her, but if she's slept this long, I won't have to worry about what she's up to while I'm at work.*

*I didn't mean to, but between forgetting to set an alarm and almost being late, I lost track of time and forgot to say goodbye to her as I left for work. When I jogged up the stairs, I peeked at her closed door at the end of the hallway and nodded to myself. Deciding not to wake her to risk her mood at me being in her room uninvited, I headed back down the stairs and grabbed my keys and tote bag. I filled my stainless tumbler with ice water, and as I got into my car in the garage, I watched the door lift while my mind wandered.*

*I couldn't shake the awkward sensation that I was forgetting something. I patted my pockets and glanced around, but I had my phone, my water, my wallet, my keys. Shrugging, I thought about Mom and hoped today would be a good day. How could it not? They added new episodes of The Great British Baking Show.*

# Chapter Seven

# Clif

One minute she's laughing, and then she's taking advantage of the fact that I don't know what the fuck is going on anymore. She runs to the front of the car and throws the driver's side door open, rushing to close it behind her when she must realize three very important things simultaneously. One, the keys are not in the ignition because they're in my pocket. Two, I've got the edge of the door in my hand. And three, the best part, there isn't anywhere for her to go out here.

She tries to scream, and honestly, I've fucking had it with her and the whole world at this point so I reach in the car to grab her. With both of her wrists in one of my hands, I use the other to pull the knife out of my pocket and hold it to the vein on the side of her neck that's pumping rapidly. When I catch her gaze, she looks rabid and strung out. Her breathing increases and she starts to panic when she can't move. The sheen of sweat that's glistening off of her neck and face tells me she might be having a panic attack, but it's confirmed when her hands go clammy and she stops squirming.

Before I can say anything to reassure her I'm not trying to fucking kill her, her eyes roll back and she slumps forward in the seat. I sigh with relief for the small lucky moment to think about what the fuck I'm going to do with her. From what it looks like, she is out searching for her mother who is in fact not missing because she's dead in the trunk and has been for who knows how long. Maybe it's a money grab. Maybe this isn't even her daughter. Maybe she's an old lady serial killer. Without knowing how much time I have to act, I push her into the passenger seat and buckle the seatbelt around her.

Looking around the car and going through her purse, I try to find anything I can to help me control the situation that's so clearly out of my fucking control. I thought about leaving her there and calling the cops, but the only thing that stops me is the idea that maybe there's a way I can use the information against her. She's in deep shit. I'm in deep shit. This could work out even better than leaving her out here and stealing this junker. I can't help but look at her as her head lays to the side, her red hair covering her face and the blood dried on her forehead. She looks insane, but scared. If she murdered that woman, why is she so scared?

I pull her wallet out of the small tote on the floor and as she starts to stir, I think fast and bind her wrists with the long pink charging cord plugged into the dash's USB. I watch as she slowly blinks to get her bearings on where she is and what's going on, and what kind of situation she's in. Then, I pull out her driver's license to get a good look at her. Her photo must not have been taken that long ago since she looks about the same now. Copper hair past her shoulders, hazel eyes, just shy of 5 feet tall and about 115lbs, but it's the name that gets me. She groans when she rotates her head to look me in the eyes and all I can think is a silent plea that she doesn't fucking puke. I hate puke.

"Sonnet," I say out loud just to hear the name in the night air. It's an interesting name for what appears to be a very unique woman, for lack of a better word. The look she gives me says she's not in the mood, but that's too fucking bad since now we're both in this mess. Her attitude is infuriating. It would get on my nerves if she wasn't so...I don't know. Cute is too sweet, but she's something. Alluring, maybe. Like a little siren since those are also hot chicks that have blood on their hands. "Sonnet Elizabeth Franklin."

"W-who are you?" she groans in response. I can tell she's angry, but she's desperately trying to appear compliant with her best impression of a sweet girl. Maybe she thinks it'll work because she's pint sized, but I can't unsee the sight of her having a full on American Psycho moment back there. "What have you d-done to my mother?"

My reflex reaction is to laugh, but I look at her curiously and my eyes narrow when I try to read her intentions. "Now, now, Killer, don't try to pin this one on me. Whenever that broad kicked it, I promise you I have an alibi," I say to her and she snarls like a little beast. "Try again."

She straightens in her seat, pulling at her bound wrists and huffs to blow her hair out of her face, but it keeps falling. Before I can stop myself, I reach over and brush it out of her eyes and she snaps. The little bitch actually tries to bite me. "Just fuck off, Jack. Ok? I have to finish this. I'm running out of time now."

"Jack?" I ask with confusion as she tries unsuccessfully to free her wrists. All she manages to do is use the side of her arm to wipe some of the blood from her face. It doesn't make her look less sexy and terrifying at the same time. Sexy? Shit, I mean. Well, it's true. I bet she looks like a straight up stunner out of scrubs, even though I kinda have a thing for nurses ever since I saw that Blink-182 album cover.

"Yeah, Jack. You car-jacked me and I don't care what your name is because I just need you to let me go before we're both in trouble," Sonnet says to me annoyed like we're just a couple friends running late for dinner reservations. Her lips curl and I can't help but look at them. When I do, she looks right back at mine.

"Killer, I'm in trouble for being a couple stacks short at hold 'em, you're in a whole different kind. And my name is Clif," I tell her with more flirtation than is necessary. Actually no flirtation is necessary, but I don't know what's come over me because this is not a date, but I'm grinning at her like a fucking idiot. She doesn't look like anyone I've met before, but it could be the lack of sleep, food, and pussy. If we'd just been two people sitting at the bar ordering Jack and Cokes from Charlene, I wonder how much of her she'd let me touch. Snapping me out of it, she laughs.

"Well, *Clif*, we're in deep shit," Sonnet says with a giggle that turns quickly into a few tears. I don't know what to do with her or how to handle anyone's emotions. Shit, I don't even have a handle on my own since all I know how to do is drink and play cards when I'm pissed. "Just call the cops on me then. It's whatever. You came for money, right? Take it."

She nudges her tote bag on the floor with her sneaker, and I can tell she has the whole world on her shoulders. I shouldn't give a shit, and part of me doesn't, but the selfish side says there's a way we could both benefit from what happened tonight.

# CHAPTER EIGHT

## Sonnet

I'm stuck in my own car in the middle of the desert with a guy named Clif who has a knife to me. As my memories of the past 24 hours start to war in my head between what's real and what's not, and what I remember doing and what I don't, I cough to clear my throat. I still haven't eaten anything, and now I'm in a much deeper hole than I realized. With the world crashing in and pulling me to the current moment in reality, I look over at him and realize that he's made no attempt to hide his face or his name from me. From everything I've learned, that makes my outlook grim and I start to panic again.

He's tall, with unnaturally bright blue eyes umbrellaed by thick black brows that match his hair, and what looks like a busted lip. If he's already been violent tonight, he might not stop with me regardless of what it looks like happened to my mother. He watches me nudge my canvas tote over to him on the floor, but he doesn't try to move. He looks right through me in an unnerving way that makes me feel his gaze on my skin like the brush of his fingertips.

"I don't think you have the kind of money in there that I need, Killer," Clif says with a smirk. I can't help my eyes from going right to where his lips curve. There's a slight cut there that looks like it's stopped bleeding, but the rough look suits him for some reason. Oh my god. I can't be thinking like this right now. I know panic and extreme stress does this, but how soon before you can start experiencing Stockholm's? I really am crazy.

"Stop calling me that. I didn't kill her," I assert, but we both hear the uncertainty in my voice as I break eye contact with him and look away. "It doesn't even matter anymore anyway. My life is over."

"Sonnet, listen to me," he tells me, but I don't look at him. I fidget, but I'm not scared of him exactly. I'm more scared of what I've done. Might have done. This is a death penalty state and if I'm caught with my dead mother in the trunk, it doesn't look good for me. I can't even blame it on Clif, who looks more like a criminal than I do. "I can help you fix this and you can help me, ok? We can work together and then we're both out of this shithole. But you have to snap the fuck out of it because you're right, we don't have any fucking time."

"If you're such a genius, how are you in deep shit too?" I ask sarcastically and look at him with an eye roll. I don't care if I'm being a brat, I might go down for matricide if we don't do something, so whatever he's capable of seems less concerning at the moment. "And why would I trust you anyway?"

"Killer, you don't have to trust me, you just have to know I'm highly fucking motivated to get what I want tonight," he says in almost a growl, but the slightly sexual undertone of it catches us both off guard. He leans in toward me just a little, like he's testing me to see how much he intimidates me. I'm not going to let him see my fear, so I don't pull back. I hold firm and grind my back teeth to stay strong.

"...What *do* you want from me, Clif?" I wonder out loud, but it sounds more sultry than I intended because the moment the words escape my lips, I can feel my eyes widen. The corners of his mouth curl and I can't help but follow the movement of his tongue as it slowly traces the raised metallic cut on his lower lip. For a split second, I completely lose concentration.

"I want you to tell me how the fuck that old woman got into the trunk so we can handle it. Then you're going to drive me to your house on 5657 Revello Circle and we're going to find some of Mommy Dearests' jewelry or something so I can pay my debt," he tells me while he curls a piece of my hair around his fingertips, lightly brushing his tattooed knuckles against the cup of my bra. "Capisce, Sonny?"

As he awaits my verbal confirmation of compliance, he narrows his eyes to scan every part of my face like he's trying to read me. When I give him nothing, he grazes my breast with a little more intention. I don't know if he's trying to rattle me or feel me up, but either way, living with my mother for the past couple years must have turned me into a touch-starved alley cat because my back involuntarily arches ever so slightly and I pray he doesn't notice. I thought it would come off intimidating, but I don't think that's what the look on his face says.

"So you help me, I pay you, then what? I've seen your face," I whisper as he continues and I imagine what it would feel like with no barrier between us. The car feels like a bubble and in it, we're not criminals or strangers. Maybe this is just how my body is trying to survive. "Tell me the truth, Jack."

"Truth, huh? Ok, fine. Here's the whole truth, I really don't want to hurt you, but if you make me, I fucking will because I'm on a deadline and it's more than just me on the line. I'm trying to save myself so I can get my little brother out of jail. I have people after me and I saw you at the station, figured I could take your car, take your money, and convince you to help me get more. I'm on a time limit. That's all it is, Killer. I just need the cash. I can't help my brother if I'm in the cell next to him, you get me?" Clif explains and I start to relax knowing he doesn't intend on taking anything from me except money. For now.

"If you don't stop trying to feel me up, I'm going to put you in the trunk right next to her," I say with a snarl. My traitorous body might love the attention it's getting, but I have more important things to do than whatever that would have led to.

"Suit yourself, Killer," he shrugs and backs up, leaving me alone in the seat while he adjusts the rearview mirror. "At least tell me what she did to deserve it so I don't cross you either."

I try to recall every detail, but as it plays in my mind, it's like I'm watching it out of my body or on a movie screen in fragments. I remember it, but like it happened to someone else. There are pieces of time missing, I know that much, so I try to walk through it slowly. Might as well vent to a stranger. It's not like I can do anything else at this point.

"She's always been...harder on me because I'm not what she want-ed. She wanted a pageant kid and I just wanted to read about elves and dragons...when Dad died, part of her died too, and then she got sick. I moved in with her to take care of her because she refused the nursing home...I thought...I thought I could handle it, but last night...she tried to poison me and I snapped, I guess," I admit. I recall the satisfied look on her face the moment I lifted the fork to my lips. The moment she thought she rid herself of her greatest regret. Losing myself in thought, a tear escapes as I continue. "I was going to take her to the hospital, but she wouldn't stop...when she ran into the garage, I didn't know why. Then I realized she had keys, and I chased her and wrangled her into my trunk because I didn't know what else to do. I was going to drive her somewhere, but it's like I blinked and then it was this morning. I went to work and forgot...I forgot she was in there until you opened it."

"Fuck," he blurted. We sit there in silence for a moment and he shakes his head. "That's self defense becau-"

"-not anymore. If I would have just called the cops on her, they could have handled this, but I put her in there. Now she's dead and there's a silver alert issued. I can't save myself with that anymore. It's too late," I say with a shrug. Feeling bare after revealing everything in a chaotic and embarrassing overshare with a man that I shouldn't think is remotely attractive, I look over to him to find he's already staring, but I can't decipher the look he's giving me. He nods, reluctantly agreeing with me.

"Listen, we're both going to get what we want out of this because we don't have another option," he states plainly like he has a magic solution to our problems. "Now, first thing...wait..."

I see it at the same time he does. His eyes squint as he looks up at the rearview mirror. On the deserted road we're on off the interstate, a set of headlights approaching starts to fill the inside of the car with light.

# CHAPTER NINE

## Clif

"**S**hit," I say at the exact same time she does. Looking at each other to prepare for the worst, I'm at least thankful the fucking trunk is shut.

"What do we do?" she asks frantically, and shoves her tied wrists in my face. "Untie me, I'll talk to them. I look more trustworthy than you do."

"I got a better idea, Killer," I reply with a low voice as we hear the car quickly approaching, looking like it's going to pull up directly behind us. I barely give her time to think before I reach over to click the seatbelt release and lift her out of her seat. I'm lucky she's got a small frame because she instantly starts to fight me.

Wrapping her wrists around my neck, her hands settle near my hair against the back of my head like they were meant to. I pull her onto my lap with her legs bent to straddle me on the seat. The light from the car behind us moves to the side as they line up to park directly next to my door.

"Kiss me, Sonny," I whisper to her while I snake one hand up the back of her scrub top against her soft skin. The other is in her hair, pulling her head toward me to nudge her a little. At the guidance, she gives me one direct look into my eyes as she contemplates. As I hear the car stop, I realize we're out of time. "Fuck it," I say as I drag her lips to mine.

The second our mouths crash together, I move to part her lips with my tongue and she doesn't stop me. I don't know if it's for show, but she also doesn't stop me from flattening my hand on her back or moving up to where her bra clasp sits. As she leans into our kiss, I adjust my hips, slightly pushing upward into her and she lets out the smallest, briefest moan, and it makes me want to discover every little noise I can pull out of her.

I let myself block out everything just for a moment when I feel her body move, but I don't close my eyes and neither does she. When a knock on the window breaks the silence, I look to the asshole that ruined this for us as she buries her head into my neck on the opposite side and I can feel her squirm to sober herself and hide the gash on her forehead.

"Ope, looks like you kids are alright," the old man wearing a red trucker hat says with a smile that I return. "Thought you might need gas or a spare tire, son."

"No, sir. Just a little minx that couldn't wait til we got home," I say with a wiggle of my eyebrows as I shamelessly bring my hand down from her back to grab her ass. "You know how they get."

"The wife used to be like that, especially when she was knocked up," the man laughs. "You kids be careful now. It's dangerous out here." With a tip of his head, he turns to walk back to his truck.

We don't move until the dirt and gravel kicks up and his taillights fade away to bring the darkness back to us. There's a small calm the minute before it happens where I can still feel her warm breath under my ear and her flexible body in my hands. Just as I inhale to take in the smell of her fear seeping through her jasmine perfume, Sonnet lifts her bound wrists over my head and uses them to push back at me while she squirms to get off of my lap.

"Ugh. Get the fuck off me and untie this," she huffs with disgust as she pulls back to thrust her wrists in my face, but I smile deviously knowing she's full of shit and I can't help myself.

"Fine, sweetheart, but don't act like you weren't two seconds away from riding my c-" I start and drag her hips down onto me. She shoves me in the chest and makes a face that was probably supposed to feign disgust, but it looks adorable when she's trying to convince herself of a lie her body can't hide.

"-bullshit, asshole. You're not my type. We have more important things to do than flirt and lie to ourselves," she says the last part a little quieter, and we both still. She's half right. We have to make a plan to handle this as quickly as we can so we can both get out of the life-ruining disasters we're both in. I slice my knife through the cord and it falls onto my lap. "Thank you," she says softly as she slides back into the passenger seat.

I sigh and straighten my spine as I turn the keys in the ignition. She might be right that we need to handle our shit, fine, but the part about me not being her type? We'll see about that. Pulling back out onto the road, I look over at her. She seems to be calmer and more alert, but I know exhaustion when I see it.

"Why don't you eat some of the food you bought, ok? It's going to take a little bit to get to the spot where I'm going to...stop," I say carefully. I don't know how upset she is about what happened with her psycho mother, but the last thing I need is her passing out again.

As she nods and leans down to pick up the plastic bag from BP, my stomach growls to remind me I'm fucking hungry too.

"Here, we can share," she offers, ripping her Slim Jim in half and handing one side to me. For another few miles, we just eat in silence. We still have a long night ahead of us.

# Chapter Ten

## Clif, Age 17

*T*he first night of Dad's sentence in the pen, Joey and I sat at home without even knowing what to put on tv. With him being an alcoholic after Mom died, it was only a matter of time before he did something stupid that left him with no other choice than to rot away somewhere. Apparently, the part of Mom that still lived on in us wasn't enough for him, and all it did was make him an angry piece of shit when he was around. I'm not even sad he's not coming back for my own sake, but what it did to my brother pissed me off enough to wish Dad would have gotten a lot worse than what he did.

The court gave custody of us to our Aunt Mel, but with me being almost 18, she just sent money and visited every once in a while. Joey and I always looked out for each other anyway, and it was no different than Dad being home except now we didn't have to worry about his temper and ridicule. Joey didn't have to hide his books anymore. He could read anywhere in our small shitty house, and for the first time, he read at the kitchen table.

*"I'll get something else for us to eat tomorrow, ok?" I offer when I bring over two bowls of the same generic mac n' cheese we'd eaten for the past four nights. Joey wouldn't ever complain, but he deserves better than this. We both do. He nods and turns a page. "Aunt Mel's check should be here tomorrow. Do you want a new book or anything? We can go pick one up tomorrow after school."*

*"Nah, it's ok. I don't need anything," Joey says looking up as he turns the page and eats in silence.*

*Watching him read, I feel a slight tinge of understanding. While Dad always told him to get his goddamned head out of the fantasy world, I get why he'd want to imagine being there instead of here. I don't even know where "there" is, but all I know is it has to be better than this house that still smells like sweat, booze, and dirty clothes. Now that Dad is gone, I can clean this place up for us instead of going to class tomorrow and I'll make sure Joey is ok. I know he's only five years younger than me, but I feel like the world doesn't have to harden him like it did me, and I won't let it.*

*"What's the book about?" I ask. When Joey looks up with an annoyed face at the interruption, it fades when he realizes I'm not Dad and I'm asking because I actually want to know. At the opportunity to talk about something that's important to him, his face lights up and he takes another bite of mac n' cheese before preparing me for the epic story.*

*"Ok so it's a series, and there's a lot of different kingdoms they call realms. Each one believes they have the right to rule the other, and they go to war over it sometimes with the creatures and powers they have. Some books have dragons fighting elves, but in another one it's just sorcerers against kings and queens. I don't know, maybe it's lame," he says with a self conscious shrug as he pulls the book closer to him.*

*"Dude, are you kidding? That sounds cool as fuck," I say honestly. It's one of the few times I've sworn in front of him, trying my best to keep any*

traits of our shitty father to myself, but seeing his smile widen is a light in the grim darkness we've been surrounded by in this house.

"Yeah! It's pretty cool as fuck," he says with a nod as we both share a laugh. His spine straightens and I don't know how, but he looks like a kid and a teen at the same time. He's my baby brother, but right now, he looks older. Maybe he just needed room without the threat of being at the heavy hand of our asshole dad. This is what Joey looks like when he's safe.

"Read it out loud then," I suggest. When he starts to shrink, I remind him of the obvious. "It's our house now, bud, we can do whatever the hell we want and I say the new rule is we read books out loud at the table."

"You really want to hear it?" he asks with a smile dipped in the most hope I've ever seen on his face. He's almost inhaled the small bowl of cheesy pasta and I curse the world in my head for not having more to make, but tomorrow would be better. At least, I can give him this, and honestly, I won't lie. It might be nice to escape to this fantasy world with him.

"Hell yeah," I say enthusiastically and lean back in my chair with a shrug. "We have to find out who wins the war, right?"

"Well, a huge war just ended, but this one is about what happens when there's trouble in the ranks and the Dragonborn have to fight their own," Joey answers with a tone that hints how serious it's about to get for the characters. The intensity in his voice, combined with the way he leans forward like he's sharing a secret, tells me all I need to know. Dad and I might be lost causes, but this smart kid with the wild imagination is going to be alright.

# Chapter Eleven

## Sonnet

Driving around the desert looking for a place to dump my dead mother with a broke criminal who I'm sharing gas station snacks with sounds like a page from a ridiculous old school Mad Libs book, but it's not. It's my Tuesday night. The never ending night that seems to test the very threads of my sanity, but I'm trapped in it and sinking like I'm in the deep end of a pool, but no one hears me drowning.

I look over at Clif as he narrows his eyes to focus on the road ahead. Even in the passing headlights, I can see the determined look he wears on his face like an iron mask. His scuffed up hands and the cut on his lip are the only injuries I can see, but with the way he winced when he pulled me onto his lap, I can tell he's probably nursing bruised ribs. I could take a look, but not much you can do for ribs, and I'm surprised I even care anyway. I don't. I guess I'm just always mentally at work since there's nothing else going on in my life aside from reading the adult version of fantasy books like the Dragon Princess Series I fell so madly in love with when I was a kid.

Smirking to myself, it dawns on me as to why I looked at him a little longer than I should have when he kissed me. The version of those books I read when I was in middle school had the princess slay the dragon and defeat the villain. In the books I read now, the princess and the villain ride the dragon together, and he slays anyone who dares touch her. Oh my god. I've enemies-to-lovered myself and I need to snap the hell out of it immediately. This is serious. This is real life, not a page from my latest book boyfriend saga. I'll let him help me handle things with my mother, and then I'm signing myself up for those therapy apps or maybe one of those male narrator apps. Oh my god, maybe both? Two years of caregiving and replacing books with social interaction has really done a number on me.

The click of the turn signal pulls me out of my daze and we take the exit to a quieter part of town with a few scenic parks and shops near the historic downtown. He slows his speed and I can tell he's contemplating the spot we're going to leave her, but I don't say a word. I just watch him work. I'm not sure how long he's lived here, or if he even does, but he looks around like someone who knows a lot about where we are. I wonder if he's ever come to the ER, or even his brother. Maybe I was working and didn't see him. Maybe it was my night off. I wonder if we've crossed paths in the grocery store, or if we would have eventually. Would I have even looked his way? Maybe he wouldn't have looked mine.

As we roll into a parking lot near a quiet shopping district on the outskirts of town, I look around. I actually know this spot, but I've been so over-worked that I forgot picturesque scenes like this even existed in a world full of inflation and turmoil. Clif cracks the windows and shuts off the car. When I move my hand to release the seat belt, he puts one hand over mine and the other to his lips telling me to stay quiet. I pause.

"Shhh," he motions through his lips. We wait for a moment. The only sounds that fill the silence are the cars passing by on the bridge overhead and the occasional ambulance or police siren. After a few minutes, he gives the nod of approval. "Come on. We'll put her over there."

I follow the point of his finger and I can see a wooden bench that sits near the small pond under the bridge. On a normal day, it's somewhere I'd sit and read while I watched the ducks swim around, but tonight, it's where we leave my mother's body. We walk to the trunk and pop it open, keeping an eye out for anyone nearby. When he lifts her, her head rolls and she stares through me with lifeless eyes that still seem to carry the weight of her judgment. I inhale sharply at the sight, and Clif turns to me seeing what affected my calm so suddenly. Adjusting her in his arms, her head tilts the other way and he creases his brows to assess me.

"I-I'm ok," I offer almost convincingly, even to myself. "It's ok."

"You want to wait in the car, that's fine. You don't have to-" he tries, but I can't let him do something that he doesn't need to do for me. He could have left me alone and called in an anonymous tip, but he didn't. I know he needs the money, but he could have been a lot more aggressive to get it by now. Between Clif, my mother, and myself, I can't help but think maybe *I'm* the scariest one out here in the dark.

"-I'm coming with you," I interrupt and I don't know why. I could just let him handle this, but for some reason, I feel like this is closure I desperately need and just wasn't prepared to collect. He just nods and keeps walking. I follow by his side, matching his stride as a subconscious show of unity and strength. This is happening and I can do it. I have to.

When we get to the bench, I stop. Clif looks at me as if to tell me I don't need to watch this part, but I nod in approval so he knows I won't allow myself to look away after what I've done. I need to see. I deserve to carry the memory of her death on my soul because I'm far too late to try to report a tale of self defense or temporary insanity. He lowers, wincing at the pain I knew he had in his ribs, and lays her on the bench, softly running his hand over her face to close her eyes.

"She looks like she's just resting," I say, not meaning to state the obvious, but needing to fill the silence and give myself a tiny gift of comfort somehow. I stumble a little as I try to gain my footing, and Clif puts out a hand on the small of my back to steady me, and probably to make sure I don't pass out again.

"Do...you wanna say a few words or something?" he asks with a shrug, unsure about how to handle a potentially volatile and highly emotional woman who slaughtered her mother.

For a second, I feel everything all at once and it almost knocks me off my feet. I feel the absence of my last remaining relative, the loss of the mother I wish I had, the fear of what I've done and what we're doing now, the desire to lose myself in a dangerous man to numb it all, and the sadness of what will happen when they find her. Just as quickly as it all crashes into me, I squeeze my eyes shut to blink it away and swallow down the hard painful lump in my throat. It happens in a matter of seconds, but it feels like I've been standing here in this spot for decades. Like it's my personalized circle of Dante's Inferno. Clif moves his thumb on my lower back in a slow up and down motion and it immediately grounds me back to the present, back to him.

"I don't know what to say," I whisper with a quiver to my voice. I don't let one tear fall because I don't know if I feel sorry for her or myself. Could I mourn us both at the same time? Is that wrong?

"Come on, Sonny, let's go. We can't stay here," he says, guiding me away and back to the car.

I don't even remember my footsteps. I just blink and I'm in the car, like it never happened. The mind is a powerful thing, and what it can do to protect us is a true wonder of the world. We're on the road before I know it, and when I look down, I notice his hand on my thigh where his thumb is rubbing circles. I shift in my seat, and he jerks his hand back almost like he's afraid I'll burn him.

"Where are we going?" I ask quietly, tilting the vent to bring some cold air to my face to make me more alert and less nauseous. "I should probably...go home," I say carefully, hoping I haven't misjudged how much danger I'm actually in with him.

"We need to get cleaned up," he suggests. At first, I didn't believe him, but when I look down at my clothes, I realize I'm wearing my own blood and so is he. He's right. I have spare work clothes in my back seat, so wherever we stop, I can make it fast. "How much cash do you have on you?"

"Umm...maybe a little over $200," I answer and he eyes me suspiciously. "What? I ordered a shit ton of Girl Scout Cookies from my coworker's kids." We both chuckle and it catches me off guard.

"You get the Thin Mints?" he asks playfully.

"Obviously. I'm not a monster, Jack," I laugh and although he keeps his eyes on the road, his face relaxes into a charming smirk.

"No, you're not," he says almost in a whisper. The car simmers in silence when we spot the cheap motel at the same time. The worn vacancy sign blinks red in the darkness, and when we pull in, he turns off the car and gives me a look I can't decipher. "We'll just go in and clean up so when you go back home, it looks normal. I just need enough jewelry and shit to get me square, and then I'll be out of your life. I swear. Can you promise me you'll play along? I don't want this to be any harder on us."

I truly think about his words and weigh my options as quickly as I can. If he wanted to hurt me or worse, he could have done it countless times, but he hasn't. All he wants is money, and I'm sure there's something in Mom's closet that's got good weight to it. I don't care if everything of hers is liquidated. I just want to live my life free of this whole thing. I meet his gaze and I nod.

"Promise," I say with a tight-lipped smile.

I hand him the cash and wait in the car as he walks into the lobby alone to talk to the guy behind the counter. Reading the body language and the way they both look back at the car to shrug while wearing shit-eating grins, I can only imagine what he's saying we need the room for. Idiot men and their caveman trophies. I see him hand over some cash and the clerk slips a card to him, still wearing a smile that could curdle milk.

As he struts back to the car, I straighten in my seat and grin when he holds the key up like he won something at a carnival game. Getting out, I grab my duffel bag from the backseat and my tote from the front to follow him as we walk to room #34 toward the end of the strip of red-doored rooms. At least ours is next to the vending machine.

When he slips the card into the door and it turns green, he twists the knob to let us into our room. The lights illuminate one large bed filled with rose petals and a bottle of champagne on ice on the small nightstand. Before I can say anything, he laughs.

"Jeff at the desk said they had a newlywed couple no show, so he thought we'd want this one as a free upgrade."

"I wonder how he ever thought we were a couple..." I say with a chuckle as we lock the door behind us.

# Chapter Twelve

## Clif

I know how this probably looks to her, but it's not my fault Creepy Jeff behind the desk gave us this room. Ok, it's a little my fault because I talked up how we just needed some alone time, and couldn't wait to get where we were going before we had to jump each other. I'm not going to tell Sonnet that part or she'll...I don't know, throw me in the trunk or something.

We walk in slowly and I note she's cautious of being alone with me, especially considering there's only one bed in here. She takes a seat on the chair in the corner of the room and gets her phone out of her bag. Kicking off her shoes and stretching her arms, she closes her eyes when she rolls her neck to crack it. She looks so small on that large chair, and it's kind of cute, but I look away so I don't stare. This room is already awkward enough without me gawking at the feisty little redhead.

"I'm going to make some calls to check in," she says out loud. I'm sure she's trying to reassure me, but we're still at a point where we shouldn't trust each other even if we want to. She could easily call the cops to say I pushed her into everything that happened tonight.

With one look at me, and who my father was or where my brother currently is, they'd throw me in cuffs without thinking. When she sees my hesitation, she rolls her eyes. "Fine, watch if you want, but stay quiet. I don't really know how to explain you yet."

I put my hands up in a playful surrender. "You got it, Killer. I'll be good," I say to her as I sit on the edge of the bed to watch her. I rest my elbows on my knees and try to be subtle as I stretch my side to gauge how sore I am from Walt's guys kicking my insides around before stealing my car.

Listening to her call Kathy, who sounds like a nice neighbor lady, I can hear the tired tone of her voice. At first, I thought she'd have to fake it, but she really is exhausted, and now that I sit on the bed, I am too. Even if I hadn't gotten the shit punted out of me I'd be tired as hell, but it just feels like everything in me is about to power down.

When she's finished, she tosses her phone on the small table next to us and looks at me. "Do you want me to look at your side? You obviously know I'm a nurse," she offers with a heavy sigh, gesturing at her scrubs. Normally, I would scoff and say it's no big deal, but it wouldn't hurt to make sure everything works fine. Plus, I would be a rotten fucking liar if I said the idea of her peeling off my shirt didn't do something to me.

To my immediate dismay, she doesn't peel my shirt off like I expected. She just looks at me and starts asking questions. I go through the order of events so far and spare her no details, including the part where I hopped into her backseat. When I finish, she sighs again and walks over to me. I can feel the electricity in her proximity and I don't know if it's just me, but my heart rate picks up the closer she gets.

"Sit up straight," she demands and when I obey, I realize I'm not talking to my Little Killer turned captive, I'm talking to an ER nurse that's probably seen more fucked up shit in her week at work than

I have in my whole life. She puts one hand on my back in between my shoulder blades and the other on my wrist over my pulse which is beating rapidly now with her educated touch. Looking at me seriously, she asks another series of questions.

"Can you take a deep breath for me?" she asks with the clinical voice I'm sure she uses with everyone, but the slight authority in it makes me fight like hell to keep the smirk off my face. I breathe. "Again," she instructs. I do exactly what she says. Fucking gladly.

"Is that good?" I ask just so she'll talk to me. She looks at me with narrowed eyes that search mine back and forth, seeking my intentions.

"If you're not having any sharp pains when you take a deep breath, you don't have a fever, and you're not experiencing shortness of breath I'd say overall you're probably looking at bruised ribs at the most. Of course there's no way to be sure, but that would be my guess for now. We'll keep an eye out. Are you bruised?" she asks, and looks at my black t-shirt like she can see through it somehow. I do everything I can to keep my dick from announcing my thoughts, but I don't know how I can think about baseball with her hands on me like this.

"I haven't looked," I answer honestly with a shrug. "We should make sure," I add with a small hint of false concern. Before she gets a chance to stop me, I slowly stand and stay facing the wall so she can see my side. She's probably a little over a foot shorter than me, and I can't help but notice the size difference in us the closer we get. She's a viscous little thing, but her height makes it deceiving.

She remains silent as I reach behind my head to pull the shirt off, and I let it drop to the floor at our feet. Before I get a good look at myself in the mirror, I wince at the gentle press of her fingertips on my discolored skin. Part of it is the pain on the purple blotch on my side, but the other is the way it feels to have her touch on me. The very slight scratch of her nails when she moves to litter small presses along my ribs makes me want to feel them deep enough to hurt.

I stay as still as I can so I don't spook her, but I can feel my fucking heart pounding through my chest. I don't know if it's the culmination of everything we've been through tonight that binds us, but suddenly I'm not so tired, and the idea of losing more sleep with her is all I can think about. She clears her throat, taking her delicate hands from my side as I watch her in the mirror on the wall across from me. I squint to see what's happening across her face so I don't have to move and risk ruining the closeness she's granting me. I want her as close as fucking possible, but I know if I come on too strong or too fast, I'll lose the small chance I have even now. I know this is crazy, but I can't help it.

"I...your ribs aren't broken. Everything feels...fine," she says in almost a whisper, and the fluctuation of her voice is miles apart from the triage nurse I just spoke to a moment ago. This isn't Nurse Franklin. This is Sonnet. My curious Little Killer. Watching her in the mirror, I assume she's looking at the patchwork ink all over my chest and arms, but when I clock the movement of her eyes, I'm surprised I'm wrong. Pleasantly surprised, actually, because she's not *just* looking. She's devouring me, and the heat of her stare burns through my veins with every pump of my heart.

"Sonnet," I say, but I don't know why. I don't have a plan. I'm not thinking ahead. I just want to taste any part of her on my tongue even if for now it's only her sweet name. She looks up at me and fuck, I can't stop myself from turning to her. With her chin tilted up so she can meet my eyes, I can sense the need to be seen, to be touched, to get lost and escape radiating from every part of her. I reach my hand up, careful not to move too quickly, and I touch the bloody spot of her forehead where the steering wheel connected. When she winces, I hold her chin to keep her eyes on me.

"I'm sorry for this," I admit. "I wouldn't-I've never hurt a woman…I shouldn't have done this. I was scared shitless, and maybe I still am."

Her brows crease in surprise and confusion, her eyes searching for truth deep inside mine. "You're not scared of me, Clif. You're scared of what I've done," she says as shame washes over her features, and pulls her gaze away from mine, making me instantly feel the loss of her.

"Hey, come here," I say and without thinking, I pull her right into my bare chest and wrap my arms around her. At first, I feel her entire body tense like she's going to fight me and run, but as I slowly rub her back, her muscles relax. The side of her face finds its way to my beating heart and in seconds, our breathing syncs. "You did what you had to do. There was no other way."

She's quiet for a moment, but then she whispers into my skin as she brings her palms to my stomach, slowly sliding them up my chest next to her face. "I'm scared that I won't ever feel guilty," I feel her say against me. Tilting her head up to meet my eyes, I can see the shades of green, brown, and gold. They're the camouflage she's been hiding herself behind for who knows how long, suppressing who she is. "Are you scared of me now?"

As her hands explore my chest, and move to my shoulders, I shake with the restraint I'm showing. I could slice her clothes from her body, throw her against the wall and split her in two, but for some reason, I can't…so I decide to be honest because, fuck it, might as well.

"Killer, I'm not scared of anything except the idea that you might push me away before I can touch you or taste you again," I answer, trying not to be too shamelessly desperate, but at this point I am. I want her so fucking bad I feel like I'd sell my worthless soul just to see what her body looks like under those scrubs.

She tilts her head curiously almost in challenge as her hands continue to move, but this time, they move lower. When she reaches the waist of my jeans, she traces a line along my belt and the tease of her nail on my skin elicits a growl through my teeth.

"You know, when I was a girl, I used to read this series where a princess was kidnapped by an evil prince from a rival kingdom after the queen was assassinated. It was c-"

"Are you talking about Dragon Princess?" I ask with a laugh and the look on her shocked face is one of the most priceless things I think I've ever seen. When she blushes, I pull her back into me and hold her around the waist tightly while my other hand rests on the side of her face. "My younger brother was obsessed with a few fantasy series and I distinctly remember him crushing on a Dragon Princess. Tell me about this sexy villain though," I say with a smirk as I rub her cheek with my thumb while she melts. "Did he have bruised ribs, tattoos, and a sudden thing for feisty little redhead nurses?"

"He was dangerous, but so was she," she answers in almost a warning, but god damn, I'm too far gone to heed the red flags. She could run me through with my own blade and as long as I got to taste her first, I wouldn't give a single shit. I lean in close enough to feel her breath on my lips, and sense the control over myself slip when my belt opens. "They were the only people they could trust anymore."

My restraint snaps, and I crash my lips onto hers as she pulls my jeans open. She kisses me too, but brutally, like she's been holding herself back for too long and needs a welcome disassociation. I know that's what this is for both of us, an escape, and that's ok. We need the release after everything that's happened, and I'm not fucking complaining if she wants to use me for anything she needs. In my 44 years of life, I've had women, sure, but it was effortless and just out of lazy convenience here and there. Whatever we're about to engage in, it already feels different from anyone I've ever been with. *She's* different from anyone I've ever been with. She's a wildling. A banshee.

Walking her a few steps backward, the backs of her knees touch the bed, and I separate our lips only to do what I've needed to do since I dragged her onto my lap twenty miles ago. Running my hands down her body, I grip the bottom of her scrub top and pull up to reveal a black lacy bra with dragons embroidered onto it, their bodies wrapped around her exposed nipples. It's the sexiest piece of lingerie I've ever seen. If I didn't think she was a Dragon Princess before, shit, at this point, if she told me to bend the knee and go to war, I fucking would.

"Fuck," I say without realizing it was out loud. I feel like a stupid teenager because one look at her in that sheer bra and I'm nervous, but I don't know why. *She* makes me nervous. I don't give her the chance to respond before I pull her back to me and return my lips to hers, only this time, our hands explore more boldly and with purpose. Grabbing at her scrub bottoms, I pull down just as she runs her hand under my boxers to slide them off my hips. I kick them off my ankles, never letting my hands leave the soft warmth of her skin, and unclasp her bra.

Laying her back onto the bed slowly, I pull her bottoms off, intentionally grabbing the elastic of her panties too. Looking at her laying on the red comforter with matching rose petals all around her, she looks like a painting. Her copper hair circles her head like a fiery halo and I wish I could take a picture of her like this to keep long after we settle our business and she forgets about this night and about me. I toss her clothes on the floor and pepper kisses from the inside of her ankle up to her inner thigh. She watches me with curiosity, and it leads me to think she's never been savored like this. I mean, I've never done it either, but with one look at her, I can't bring myself to rush it.

Only a few inches from her core, I kiss her thigh one more time before I put one of her legs over my shoulder to open her up to me. She starts to hesitate, but I lace my fingers through hers to pin them to the bed next to her hips. Being denied this would be the cruelest punishment I can imagine. When my lips are close enough to touch hers between her thighs, I inhale deeply to etch the scent of her arousal into my memory before darting my tongue out to taste her sweetness. Starting at her opening, I lap her up from core to clit as I move myself on the comforter to seek the friction on my desperately weeping cock. With every wave of my tongue to her center, I thrust my hips into the bed, feeling like my fucking head isn't even attached anymore. I'm a mindless fiend surviving for the sole purpose of drowning in her liquid pleasure. I know nothing else but this.

When her fingers relax in my hold and a soft moan leaves her, I slide my hands out from hers and it's like we've been fucking each other for lifetimes. She moves her nails through my hair, and grabs a handful to steer my mouth in the right direction while she grinds on my face. Every time I thrust my tongue inside of her, I can feel her start to tighten and pulse. The moment my hands are free, I plunge two fingers deep inside her pussy and she lets out a mixture of a scream and a giggle. I plan on taking my time and drawing her orgasm out, but as soon as I curl my digits, she's bucking her hips and dripping a delicious line of cum from between my fingers down her ass. I don't have a lot of experience with that type of sex, but god damn, I want to touch, taste, and fuck every part of her now.

Sliding my fingers out of her as she tries to recover from her climax, I crawl up her body to cage her in under me, and I bring my wet hand to her lips.

"Open," I command and she does without hesitation. I didn't think it was possible for any more blood to rush to my dick, but it does because fuck am I a sucker for a girl who listens. "Clean it up, Killer," I say as a challenge. I half expect her to knee me in the groin or cuss me out, but she parts her lips and sticks out her tongue slightly, waiting like the good girl she is. Sliding my fingers coated in her cum slowly into her waiting mouth, her tongue slowly dances in between them. When I pull them back out, I rub them softly on her wet lips. I groan into her mouth as I cover it with mine and lower myself on top of her, feeling eager to claim her. She moans in response to the slight nudge of my cock at her entrance, and it's a sound I hope I'll remember for the rest of my life.

"This doesn't mean-" she starts, but I run my hand down her body along the outside of her thigh before hooking under her knee to bring it up to my waist.

"Shhhh, I know, baby," I whisper over her lips between kisses. Lifting her leg higher to spread her open for me, I nudge a little more, my tip breaching her entrance. "I want you to take anything you want from me. Use me...ok, Killer?" I ask to confirm she still wants this. I would kill for it, but I need to make sure. I might be a criminal, but I'm not about forcing women into sex.

She tilts her head back and arches, bringing me a little farther into her wet warmth. She moans as her pussy starts to stretch and mold to my cock and I swear, I could burst with how fucking turned on I am right now, but it's not enough. I reach behind her neck to fist the hair at the back of her head and I drag her frenzied gaze back to me.

"Eyes, Sonnet. Give me those eyes. Stop me now if you don't want this," I say with desperation. I push a little more to earn another mewl from her that makes me fucking ravenous. "Baby, I need you to stop this because I can't. Fuck, I can't. I want this so bad."

I hover less than two inches inside her pussy, and I can feel a bead of sweat on my forehead as I use every bit of energy I have left to stop.

She stares into me and lifts her other leg to lock both behind my back as her nails dig into my ass.

"Clif, please," she begs as she uses her legs to pull me closer. "Please," she pleads and looks at me like I'm the only man she's ever seen. There's no way I'm the best she's ever had or even close. She's a stone cold 10, but with the way she's looking at me, I'm going to pretend.

"Ok, Killer, hold on tight," I warn her briefly before I push all of myself deep inside her until our hips are pressed against each other. We both gasp as our bodies adjust to each other, and I can't hold back for one more second.

I pump into her fast and hard. I know I told her to use me, but fuck, it's like my body is leading me and I'm helpless against it. It feels like a primal need to claim her in every way, and the deeper I reach inside of her, the more I want to howl at the full moon. Maybe it's the adrenaline crash, or the lack of sleep, or being hungry and dehydrated, but I'm weightless within her. I'm swimming in a sea of her scent, and wrapped warmly in a blanket of her embrace as the rose petals drift around us to the rhythm of our bodies. I suddenly understand why passion ignites world wars and inspires art. This is fucking magic and so unlike anything I've ever known.

"Sonnet," I say between her lips before I involuntarily let out a moan. I've never really been vocal during sex, but I can't help myself. She's paradise. I look into her eyes, and watch them roll back as she tilts her hips to angle me toward the spot that she needs me to touch. "What do you need? Say it and it's yours."

"I want," she starts, but I kiss her and pull out almost entirely before easing back into her. She groans with need and pleasure, and I just want to keep making her melt in every way I know how. "I want to...I want to switch."

I can't help but look at her with surprise, but she smirks and I remember she's not as she appears. She's not a small, scared little girl. She's a grown woman that's taken a human life. She's a killer. The image of her laughing at her dead mother in the trunk as blood drips down her face should make me uneasy, but for some fucking reason, it makes her look dangerous in a way I should definitely not be attracted to.

As I flip us over, I grab her hips to stay as deep inside of her as I can while she settles on top and begins to move. Her hair almost reaches her perky breasts and her nails dig into my chest as she rolls her hips slowly and exhales like she's holding herself back. This woman could slash me with an ice pick as long as I died still inside of her, I wouldn't care. She starts to increase her speed and her head rolls back while she releases a moan that almost makes me lose it right there, but I hold it.

"That's it, Killer, fuck me," I say, and god damn it, she does. Her body moves like a serpent, the need for her like venom racing through my veins, as she moves a hand to her clit. "I can't...I'm going to-" I try to speak through my own grunts.

"I'm on the pill...do it, Clif," she whispers in between thrusts. With a nod of her head, the second she brings her eyes to mine, she comes all over me. The pulse of her walls breaks my resolve, and I come with a roar right after her.

Slowly pumping in and out a few more times as we come down, she collapses on the pillow next to me. We lay there barely touching with me dripping out of her onto the rose petals surrounding us.

# CHAPTER THIRTEEN

## Sonnet

Who the fuck did I just turn into? I'm laying on top of a bed of roses next to the criminal that stole my car with the evidence of our impulsivity slowly dripping out of me. Before he can offer me a washcloth or his shirt, I carefully get out of the bed and grab my scrubs off of the floor to hold them against me. I know there's no sense in being shy now, but I didn't realize I had that type of hellcat in me. I suspected I might like things a little more exciting, but I've never been with anyone that I felt would let me off the leash without judgment. I can't believe I could have been having this type of sex my whole 30s?! I guess something like this could make up for a little lost time, right? God damn it, that was spicy.

As soon as I start toward the shower, I glance over at Clif who makes no move to hide his body and thank god, because I definitely don't mind looking. I don't know what sex means to him, but this was a welcome awakening of sorts for me. I'm sure it's hotter because it was an impulsive one-time fling, but I don't regret a second of it. If I go to prison for what happened with my mom, at least I'll be able to lie in my cell with a wild sex story. Maybe I can even trade the dirty details of it for things from the commissary. Before this, the craziest thing I'd experienced was a quickie in a dressing room, but now that I'd had this little escape, it was time to get back on the bus to reality.

"I'm getting in the shower," I tell him and he walks over to me, still naked so I can see every line of ink on his skin. When he gets close enough to touch me, he tilts my chin up to lock my gaze with his.

"*We're* getting in the shower," he corrects with a smirk, pushing me toward the small bathroom as he follows. "I can't have you running off, Killer. I have to keep an eye on you."

"You know where I live now, *Jack*. There'd be no point in running," I sass, and he playfully lands a light crack on my ass cheek. "Hey!"

"Fine, maybe I just want to keep my eyes on you because I like what I see," he says with a shrug. When I look back at him, his eyes travel up my body, making me want to pull him  inside me again. He seems to have the same thought because we barely get the bathroom door shut and the water turned on before he's pushing himself right back into me with my back against the sink.

When I've come two more times, and he's finished in hot streams along my stomach, we step into the shower together. Switching back and forth, we wash each other's hair and trade silence for stolen kisses under the water like we're lovers on a getaway vacation-not two crim-inals washing off evidence miles away from multiple crime scenes.

The squeaky turn of the shower knobs bring us both back into the current situation as we stand next to each other to dry off. Neither one of us knows what to say or how to start, but I wrap the towel around me and open the bathroom door to let the cold air in. The bubble we'd surrounded ourselves in to get lost for a little escape pops, leaving me to think about what happens now and if I'd run away from an active warrant. Stuck in my head with my thoughts, I avoid eye contact as I walk out of the bathroom with Clif right behind me.

Pulling open my duffel bag, I grab an identical pair of blue scrubs and start slipping them on as he dons the same clothes he had on when he kidnapped me. Oh my god, just the way that sounds is crazy. This *is* crazy. When we're dressed, I open my mouth to speak, but my stomach speaks for me. We both laugh at the way it breaks the solemn aura enclosing us, and I dig through my tote for a few bills from my wallet.

"I'll grab something from the vending machine outside, ok? I pinkie swear I won't run," I say with a matter of fact face so he knows I don't need to be micromanaged. The outside air, even though it's a little warmer than I'd like, might clear my head and help me think of what I'm going to say to him next.

"Please don't, Killer. I'm too tired to chase you, but I will if you make me," he answers with a grin that says he's flirting, but he's not joking. I'm the only thing standing between him and the money he needs, and he's the only thing standing between me and a life sentence or worse. I shrug and return his smile while I slip out of the room, leaving the door cracked open, to visit the vending machine near the stairs to the second floor.

Staring at the cash I have and the choices in front of me, I guess what the tattooed stranger in the room would like. We shared a few snacks from the gas station, but I don't know anything else about him other than he has a brother in prison and the face he makes when he comes. Just thinking about that last part makes me smile with a shudder, and I swear I can still feel his lips on my skin like an echo. Choosing two sodas, two bags of chips, and two bags of M&Ms for now, I look around as the silver coils spin to drop my selections into the tray below. It must be a slow night since the only cars out here are mine and a red Camaro.

Taking a deep breath as the last bag of chips hits the bottom, I reach in to grab it while I balance the other items in my hand. I tiptoe back to the room and tap the door open with my shoe so Clif can relax knowing I didn't make a run for it to leave him stranded with no car. As soon as I breach the doorway and smile at him, his eyes widen and he freezes. Before I can ask him what's wrong, I'm grabbed from behind and held against the large body of a man that smells like cigars and stale beer. I start to fight, but the second I do, the barrel of a gun is held to my temple, and I go cold. Remaining motionless, I stare into Clif's eyes and wait for his move.

"Now Clifton, it doesn't look like you're taking your debt very seriously if you're holed up here in a motel with a cheap redhead," he coos and the words ooze over me like a sickening sap. Although he's got one hand on the gun, his other is snaked around my torso, slithering closer to my breast with every breath I take. I can tell he gets off on the fear, so I give the disgusting asshole nothing. Suddenly, the idea of murdering another person doesn't weigh on my soul like I thought it would. If I had the ability, I'd throw this scumbag in my trunk next, but I don't move.

"She's *not* a hooker," Clif responds with a little too much gusto, and I sense the moment he regrets it because now it's not only the asshole's wandering palm he's afraid of. With an inhale into the side of my face like a hunting dog learning a scent, he sloppily kisses my cheek, and I want to puke at the way I suddenly feel like I need another shower.

"Means somethin' to you doesn't she? I didn't know you had a good girl like this, Clifton. We could have settled your debt so much easier with a little strawberry like her," he says in a low voice that he might have wanted to seem sultry, but instead it sounds creepy and predatory.

"Fuck off, cunt," I grit out as I buck my head back as hard as I can to connect with his nose. In a moment of pain, he howls and drops me to the floor just like the self defense class said he would. Before he can reach me, I'm already across the room in Clif's arms as he holds the same knife out that he used to steal my car.

The ogre stands up straight and laughs as the blood trickles down his face. His nose doesn't look completely broken, but I definitely got a good amount of damage in. I had to do something to get his grubby paws off of me before I barfed on the cheap carpeting. He goes to take one step toward us when something catches his eye on the chair next to the small table. Reaching into my tote bag, he removes my wallet.

"Take whatever money you want, and leave us the hell alone," I say with as stern of a tone as I can muster in the current situation. Clif slowly moves me behind him, and I hold onto his shirt as I peek around to watch what happens next.

"Oh, it's not money I want from you, Little Tart," he taunts as he opens my wallet. To my absolute horror, he pulls out my driver's license to recite my name and address out loud to us. "Sonnet Elizabeth Franklin of 5657 Revello Circle. I like that name. Sonnet. Like a little song bird...I bet I could make you sing for me."

"I have two more days," Clif grits through his teeth. "Leave her out of it."

"If Walt doesn't get paid, I'll collect your girl and your brother," he says with a smile, completely unbothered by the blood in his yellow teeth. He slips my license in his back pocket with a nod of his head in my direction. "Be seeing you, Strawberry."

As the door shuts behind him, Clif's tense shoulders relax and he kicks the dresser. I just stand there while everything catches up to me because I'm in this shitty quicksand deeper than I'd ever anticipated, and we're slowly sinking.

Before I get the chance to speak, my phone rings on the table, breaking the moment, and when I rush to it my eyes widen. Clif hurries to my side to look over my shoulder, and we both jump at the next shrill ring as the police department caller ID scrawls across the screen.

# CHAPTER FOURTEEN

## Sonnet

I almost freeze when I see the caller ID tell me that the police are on the line, but then I remember they're out looking for my mother and I have to pretend I am too. Sliding my finger across the screen to answer the call, I put it on speaker and let Clif's hand on my back ground me.

"Hello, this is Officer Cooper. Am I speaking to Miss Franklin?" The officer's voice fills the silence of the room like an intercom. I look at Clif as I speak.

"Yes, it's me. Her. Hi. Did you find my mom?" I ask, trying to walk the fine line between frantic and hopeful. They're either calling me to update me on their search, give me a lead, or-the officer's voice cuts through my racing thoughts.

"We've located Mrs. Franklin," he says slowly, almost like he's try-ing to tell me without saying the words, and I instantly understand what's happening, but I do my best to play my part.

"Oh, thank god. Well, I'll pick her up. Where are you? I could-"

"Miss Franklin, I'm so sorry to have to tell you this, especially over the phone, but your mother was found a few minutes ago. We called an ambulance to the scene, but she was unresponsive when paramedics arrived," he says, and his heavy heart resonates through his voice. Clif's hand moves in small circles on my back as I work up my breathing to continue.

"W-what are you saying?" I ask, letting my voice crack and fluctuate. Clif's eyes narrow on mine and I can sense he's trying to determine if any of this is real.

"Ma'am, my sincerest condolences, but your mother has passed. If you're closeby, I'd like to have you come and confirm her identity as soon as possible so you can start making the necessary arrangements."

"No, oh my god, please no," I wail, and begin to make the sounds of a woman in sorrow.

"I'm deeply sorry, Miss Franklin. Take your time getting here, and please be safe," he says, and I wonder how many times he's had to apologize for losses like this one in his career. He didn't rush me or interrupt as I continued to mimic a sob into the speaker.

"I-I'm on my way...t-thank you for f-finding her," I stutter and hang up the line. The moment the call disconnects, Clif and I look at each other and I can see the confusion in his eyes like he's lost, but down to follow me anywhere. It's probably just for the money, but at least now he knows I'm motivated to help him too, considering the alternative is becoming wannabe mobster Shrek's new play thing. I almost gag out loud at the thought.

"I'll go ID my mother and then we'll go to my place and you can root through her jewelry until there's enough to cover what you owe," I instruct as he stares at me nodding his head.

"I'm coming with you," he states, and before I can object, he pulls me into him. "I'm not leaving you alone for one more second for

Walt's guys to get close again. I could have fucking gutted him for touching you, Killer. I won't let it happen again."

The glare in his blue eyes as he looks down into mine, combined with the feel of his grip on my hips, tell me I couldn't deny him no matter how independent I've always been. I've never felt protected like this and his possessiveness isn't exactly a turn off. Although my personal space is vital to my comfort, having someone next to me that is focused on my wellbeing, even if it's for money, does feel really nice. I'll just have to let myself enjoy it until I allow him to clean out my mother's jewelry since that's the really only reason he's still here.

"Fine, but we have to motor. I don't want to give anyone the impression that I wasn't in a hurry to find her. I'll text Kathy on the way," I say plainly as I slip out of his hold with a small squeeze of his hand and start gathering my things. I can't help but stare at the state of the bed that we didn't even sleep in. I knew we wouldn't be returning now that Walt, whoever that is, knew where we were. We can't exactly stay at my house either until the payment is made since the SHEIN version of My Cousin Vinny knows my damn address by heart now.

"Good, I'm ready when you are," Clif says as he reaches onto the floor to pick up the vending machine snacks I dropped. "You got the peanut M&Ms, my favorite."

Hopping in the car while he eats handfuls of candy at a time, we drive to the police station and I try to think of how I'll explain his presence with me if I'm asked.

Standing next to a table with my mother under the cover, I already know what I'll see when it's lifted. I steel my expression as my eyes adjust to the lighting. I still haven't slept, and the sun will probably begin its ascent while we're standing here in this room. From adrenaline crashing to simple exhaustion, I'm trying not to sway on my feet, but it feels like I've been running on fumes for hours.

"I'll give you both a minute," the coroner says as he tightens his lips into a straight, sympathetic line. Giving Clif a nod when he laces his fingers through mine, the door shuts as he exits, leaving us alone with my mother.

"Sonnet, I can do this for you if you want…you don't have to look, ok?" he offers just above a whisper as his thumb traces circles on the back of my hand.

"You don't have to do that in here. No one's watching us," I reassure him as I pull my hand from his.

Before he can reach for me again, I pull the sheet down from her face just to get this over with, but when I do, the sight of her stills me. She doesn't look like the evil queen that wanted my heart in a box. She doesn't look bulletproof or fueled by resentment anymore. With her face vacant of all tension and expression, she just looks like the shell of an old woman. There's nothing there anymore. I don't know why it throws me off, but I surprise myself when my eyes begin to well. Flipping the sheet back over her, I feel tears begin to claw their way up my throat. Panicking, I turn to run from the room, and from everything waging war inside my head and my heart.

I don't even make it two steps before I'm enveloped in the warmth of Clif's body. He wraps one arm around my frame and the other cradles my head to his chest. I fight his hold for a moment, but he just rocks us back and forth.

"Hey hey. You're ok, baby, you're ok," he whispers into my hair. I can only resist for a second before I hug his waist and release everything I've been carrying inside of me for decades. I want to feel strong, but right now in his arms, I find solace and peace in putting down the heavy baggage that's been strapped to me my whole life. It's over. She'll never be able to hurt me again.

When the coroner comes back into the room with Officer Cooper, I barely make out the brief muffled conversation he has with Clif before I'm being led out of the room with his arm around my shoulders. My eyes feel swollen, and someone should invent a new word for exhausted because whatever I am right now is so far beyond that. Even walking to my car feels like I'm out of my body and watching everything happen around me.

Clif takes the keys from my hand, and helps me into the passenger seat. Leaning over me, he buckles my seatbelt and looks into my eyes, searching for answers I don't know how to find right now. As he gets into the driver's seat, he starts the car, but leaves it in park to face me.

"You need to sleep, but Walt's guys have your address. I think we should think about a hotel until..." he trails off. I know what he's thinking because it's the only reason why we're still connected at all.

"Until I give you a way to pay them, I know," I finish for him, and he looks away. "Just pick a hotel and use any credit card from my wallet. I don't give a shit anymore."

"Look, I'm sorry, ok? I'll be out of your life as soon as I can," he snaps, turning the key and pulling out of the parking lot.

After almost a half hour of awkward silence, we pull into a hotel and he parks at the entrance, flipping on the hazards. Without even asking, he leans down to grab my wallet, picking a random credit card like I told him to. Taking a card and shoving it into his pocket, he shuts the car door leaving me inside alone to stew in whatever emotion this is.

# CHAPTER FIFTEEN

## Clif

I leave her moody ass in the car for this part, and I head inside to get us a place to crash. I don't even try to get us a room with two beds. She can fucking deal with it because I'm not letting her run from me or treat me like shit because she's not happy about her bad decisions. She may not have gotten herself carjacked, but she wouldn't have been out there at all in the line of danger if she hadn't resorted to manslaughter.

I know there's a world of emotions bubbling up in her, but I can't let her fuck this up for me because it's not only me on the line, it's Joey too. When I hop back into the car and park, I turn to face her, but she takes the opportunity to get out and shut the door with a little more force than necessary. Great, so she's set on being a fucking brat then. Fine, if she wants to act like one, I'll treat her like one.

I get out of the car and fling her duffel bag and tote over my shoulder before she can grab them. When she tries to take them from me as we walk into the hotel, I hold them back and nudge her forward to keep moving. The look she gives me is lethal, but I'll take it. I'll take whatever is too much for her. I think that until the little demon pops her elbow back to poke me directly in my bruised rib, causing a sharp pain to radiate through me down to my toes. That's it. As soon as we reach the hallway, I rush forward and lift her, throwing her  over my shoulder. She tries to fight to free herself from my hold, but with one loud crack on her ass, she freezes in shock.

"You spanked me!" She shouts, her voice sounding almost disembodied as her head bobs at my back.

"Yup, and if you can't behave, I'll do it again. Knock it off, Killer. I mean it," I say to her as we near the door to our room. The second she sees there's only one bed in here, she's going to lose her shit, but I won't exactly shy away from another excuse to spank her little ass again.

"Ow, ok fine," she says with a wriggle. I'm sure it still stings, so I reach up to rub the pain. For a split second, I feel her arch her ass to my touch, but when she realizes what she's done, she squirms until I put her down.

Sliding the key card into the door, she cuts in front of me to open it and I let her discover the surprise on her own. Waiting for the temper tantrum, I'm thrown when all she does is kick off her shoes and hop into the bed. She lays her head in the mountain of pillows and stretches out before pulling the blanket over herself. It's adorable and a welcome change from the brat she was before I spanked her. Maybe that's all she needed. I drop the bag and tote on the floor, slipping off my shoes next to hers. As I put my knee on the bed to slide in, she turns to stop me.

"You're *not* sleeping in here with me. There's a couch right there," she says with her eyebrows drawn, and I know she's not playing this time. I don't know what she's worked up about now, but I guess it's easier to blame me than to look in the mirror.

"Fine, Killer," I say like it doesn't bother me in the slightest, and I go to the couch to make myself at home.

"I paid for this room so at least I get a say in this. What happened before was a mistake," she hisses and rolls over.

I look at the back of her copper head and I let her win this one. Sure, she paid for the room, but I know she's saying everything else just to make sure I hurt like she does. I squeeze my tall frame onto the couch, and it's not actually that bad. I've slept on plenty of couches, and much more uncomfortable places too, so by the time I pull the throw blanket over me, I'm out.

I wake up to the smell of bacon and coffee, and for a second I think I'm still dreaming, but when I open my eyes, she's there. Stretching my cramped legs on the couch, I yawn and sit up to see she's already eaten and there's a covered plate next to hers that hasn't been touched. Her coffee is almost empty and her thumbs move at lightning speed over her phone screen.

"What time is it?" I ask, standing and lifting my arms over my head to move my stiff muscles. She doesn't even look up from her phone as I approach the small table she sits at.

"Almost 1pm," she answers. She's talking to me like we're nothing more than strangers on a train, but I don't let it derail what we've been through together. "Hurry up and eat something so we can get this over with."

I let her boss me around for a little bit since I know she's just trying to find control in this whole situation where she's most likely spiraling behind those hazel eyes. The coffee isn't as warm as I wish it was, but I welcome the caffeine and late breakfast. We're both wary and anxious to resolve my half of the dilemma we're in, so I inhale as much of the food as I can in ten minutes or less and head to the bathroom.

I can hear her make a few calls and from the bits and pieces I've gathered, I learned a few things. First, her mother's body has been released to the funeral home and will be cremated soon. Next, she's off work for a while to deal with handling her mother's affairs - bereavement. The worst of it however is that a photo of her with her mother has aired on the local news sharing that the body of a beloved resident found near the water has been identified as Gloria Franklin. I can only imagine how pissed she is that something so personal is now the talk of her job, her neighbors, and anyone else that takes a local neighborhood tragedy to pretend they knew the family for attention.

When we get in the car to head for her house, she's a different version of Sonnet. This version isn't outright bratty, but she's passive aggressive as fuck. I even brake-checked a car behind me just to see her react to something, but no luck. She stares at her phone and scrolls through Instagram until we pull into her driveway.

When I turn off her car, she stops to look up for the first time since we started driving from the hotel, reigning in her surprised expression at my knowing which house was hers. I can see the moment she remembers I saw her ID and so did Walt's guy, because she looks annoyed and frustrated. I follow closely behind her as she unlocks the door and we walk into the last place her mother was seen alive.

"Mom's room is upstairs and her jewelry box is on her dresser. Take whatever the fuck you want and I'll drop you off at wherever you need to go," she motions up the stairs while she moves to what must be the basement door. "I'm going to my room to change and grab more clothes. Make it quick."

Before I get the chance to speak, she's gone. I sigh and walk up the stairs to find what I came here for. The house is eerily quiet and the top stair creaks when my foot covers it. To my left, there's a bathroom, and to my right, the hallway shows two doors. I walk toward them and when I pass the first, it looks like a home office. I lean in to look around and it appears oddly untouched, almost like whoever worked here just quit and never collected their things. There's an outdated computer on the desk in front of the window and the walls are lined in bookshelves. I stay in the doorway, feeling like it's a sacred space I shouldn't be in, but I narrow my eyes to read some of the book's spines. Based on the room, I assumed the books will be reference or nonfiction, but upon closer observation, they're not, they're mostly fantasy.

A soft smile creeps over my face. If this was her father's space, it makes sense why she grew up loving books like the Dragon Princess series. Snapping out of the memory that doesn't belong to me, I turn my focus to the large bedroom at the end of the hall. When I enter that one, it becomes immediately evident that this is Gloria's space. It looks like a model home, cold with nothing out of place. The bed is made, there are pink roses in a crystal vase on the nightstand, and when I look at the open door of the closet, the clothes are all sorted by color and length. If you were to tell me it was staged by a realtor, I'd believe you. There's not one family photo anywhere. No trace of a daughter in any part of it.

I feel a small unwelcome pull in my chest for my Little Killer. Her mother clearly doesn't radiate any fucking warmth or maternal instinct if this room is any representation of what she was like. I walk to the wall next to the closet door and just as Sonnet said, there's an ornate silver jewelry box on the dresser. When I open it, it's all organized and displayed like the Hope Diamond. Even just a few of these things could clear my debt, so I choose the biggest ones in an attempt to take the least amount of items I can.

Sliding the three rings into my pocket, I carefully close the box and exit the room. With one more curious look into the office on the way back to the stairs, my eyes scan the desk to find a small framed photo of what must be little Sonnet with her father. They look to be at a renaissance faire or something because they're dressed in medieval clothes and she's proudly clinging to a book. I've never had the best experience with having a healthy family, but I don't have to be an expert to see the amount of love in that small 4x6 photo. At least it seemed like her dad loved her enough to almost make up for whatever she didn't get from her bitch of a mother.

When I walk down the stairs, it's empty in the living room and kitchen, but the basement door is still open. I contemplate waiting on the couch, but with the undying curiosity that continues to fuck me over in my life, I can't help myself. As quietly as I can, I tiptoe gently down the few stairs to her sanctuary, knowing this is the best chance I have to see the most raw version of who she is instead of who she pretends to be.

At the step before the last, I see her before she sees me. She's sitting on her bed wearing a casual dress and looking through the contents of a shoebox. She looks so small. I have to remind myself what she's really capable of because right now in this light, she's just a broken little girl inside that body. I open my mouth to speak, but her head snaps to me and the vulnerability in her glassy eyes is impossible to hide.

Quickly swiping the tears from her cheeks, she puts the shoebox back under her bed and grabs her freshly packed duffel bag to stride past me. The moment she's in arm's reach, I pull her to me and she doesn't get the chance to fight me off. She looks right into my eyes and it's like she's waiting for something, but neither of us knows what.

"Sonnet, I-" I start, but she doesn't let me finish.

"Did you get what you came here for?" she asks with a bite and I grip her shoulders tighter.

"If I don't get the money, they'll come for you, me, and my brother. If there was any other way, I'd find it. I'm not going to let anything happen to you, ok? I don't want to hurt you, Killer," I confess honestly. I'll still have to sell what I got, but at least I know the shit with Walt will be finished. If she thought I was just going to bail after, she's wrong. I don't know what we're doing, but whatever it is, I'm nowhere near done with her.

"Get me out of this house then," she says in almost a plea. Her softness stills me. "Please."

When she whispers that word into the silence, I take the duffel bag off of her shoulder and put my hand in hers. In less than two minutes, we're back in the car on the way back to the hotel with my hand on her thigh, and her dead mother's jewelry in the front pocket of my jeans.

# Chapter Sixteen

## Sonnet

I know I've been an asshole to Clif, but I don't know what to do about it. I can't apologize because on some level, I'm not exactly sorry. I can't thank him for holding my secret and helping me out of trouble because it wasn't out of the kindness in his heart - he stole from me for payment. As soon as he pays those shady people, then he'll leave and I'll figure out what I want with my life now that I don't have my mother to tell me how I fucked it all up for her and myself. I don't hate him...I just don't want it to be meaningless. I don't want to be meaningless anymore. I want to matter to *him*.

When we get back to the hotel, I remember I told him I'd give him a ride to settle his debt, but he doesn't bring it up so neither do I. As soon as we walk into the freshly cleaned room with the remnants of breakfast and a messy bed gone, I turn to him to speak, but all I can think of is how cruel I was to him. I'm not sorry for all of it, but some of it wasn't warranted. I did lie. When I told him that being with him was a mistake, I didn't mean it was mine. The riptide of an ocean full of warring emotions keeps pulling me from current to current, and now that I'm lost at sea, the only time I remember feeling sane in the past 72 hours has been when I was in his arms.

"Clif," I say quietly as we stand in the middle of the room. He turns to look at me and I can see something in his blue eyes I missed before. The ocean I'm wading water in. I'm not as alone in it as I thought. He looks at me, waiting to hear what I have to say, and suddenly I can see his exhaustion, his fear, his remorse...and his desire. "I'm sorry."

"Why are you apologizing to me?" he asks with an honest face as he puts both hands on my hips, making my black sundress ride up just a little. He's not asking to hear me list my wrongs, he's genuinely curious as to why I'm offering it at all. I put my hands on his upper arms to brace myself, and I let the subconscious part of my mind speak.

"I know you have to do this. It's not personal. I hope you clear your debt for you and your brother, and if you need more, you can have it. It's not like she'll need it now anyway, and ...I...I guess I want to help," I answer him, and as I speak, his thumbs move to ease my anxiety. "At least what I did wrong can do some good before you go."

"Shhh..." he quiets me and my mind shuts off too. "I'll be here as long as you'll let me." He let the words slip out mindlessly, and just as I think he'll regret them or take them back, the opposite happens. He looks into my eyes and there's relief. "Is that it, Killer? You're not done with me?"

I narrow my eyes at him, annoyed momentarily that for some reason to him, I'm so easily read. He's right. I don't want to be alone right now, and he's the only person in the universe I know of that can understand me and give me what I need. Instinctively, I want to be a smartass to him, but when he grips me harder and with clear intention, I don't.

"I don't know what I want," I admit honestly. It makes me feel chaotic and emotionally disorganized, but it's the truth. Looking up at him as he leans lower, his lips curve into a devilish grin like I'm the food he likes to play with. "I-"

"-I know what you need. Lift your dress for me, Killer," he says in a breathy tone right over my lips. "Slowly," he instructs, his hands never leaving my hips as he keeps his close proximity.

I hesitate, then rest my hands at my sides, using the curl of my fingers to grab a handful of the fabric. I lift it higher and higher up my thighs. My racing mind begins to quiet like there's nothing happening in the entire galaxy except this right now. I can feel the front of him tent against his jeans, and I keep lifting until the purple thong I have on is completely exposed. Staying still, I wait for the next direction, enjoying how good it feels to be told what to do while my brain powers down and my basic instincts take over.

"Very good, Little Killer. Now...stay," he commands.

I follow his eyes as they stay locked on mine. He lowers his body to his knees and with a grin, he hooks his fingers around the band of my panties, pulling them down my legs at a frustratingly glacial pace. When I open my mouth to speak, he shakes his head and puts a finger over his lips to silence my attempt. Tapping my ankles one by one, he helps me step out of the little strip of purple lace. Looking right through me, he puts it in his pocket.

While I stand there holding my dress to my hips, I shiver as the cool air conditioning in the room makes me even more aware that I'm completely bare to him from the waist down. He leans closer to my core and I brace myself for the warm flat of his tongue as I close my eyes and tilt my chin up. When it doesn't come, I look down to find him inhaling me and I war within my mind between feeling turned on and embarrassed. With lungs full of my scent, he raises to his full stature leaving me confused and struggling to steady my breath.

He walks backwards slowly to the couch and when I try to follow, he puts a hand up to signal that he wants me to stay. I'm fighting the humiliation as it creeps in while he sits, spreading his legs and unbuttoning his jeans. The sound of his zipper is deafening, and I watch as he frees himself, holding one hand to his shaft while the other rests behind his head. He shamelessly delivers several slow strokes to his hardened cock and all I can do is stare at how beautiful he is.

"Touch yourself for me, Killer," Clif says, his velvet voice tickling the inside of my ears from where he sits. I start to fidget because this is so much more sexy and vulnerable than anything I've ever done, but when I read about it, it's hot as hell. I want to do whatever he tells me to, but I'm nervous. What if I don't look sexy? What if I can't get there with him watching? As if he can sense my spiraling apprehension, he reacts.

"Sonnet, slide your fingers into your pussy and let me see how wet you are...now."

His words pull at me like marionette strings, and I keep my dress at my waist in one hand while the other ventures lower. His breathing deepens with mine and he watches closely as I glide over my clit and sink my middle finger inside myself. Drawing it back out, I trail my wetness back to my bud to circle it before sliding it through my lips and back inside. I've touched myself countless times in my own bed, but this feels incredible. My insecurity and need to control the situation fades, and I'm not timid like I thought I'd be. It feels powerful to see the effect I have on him as he watches me and strokes himself.

"Two fingers," he groans and I obey, adding another into my core while he increases his speed. I try not to think about it, but I'm already close enough to feel my toes dangling over the edge of my climax. All I want to do is dive in, but I'm not ready for this to end. I let out a moan and the fingers gripping my dress whiten at the knuckle as my hips begin to move with my speed. "Don't you dare come," he snaps and it pulls my eyes right to his.

"But, Clif," I whine, and he gives me a look that stops me. I keep my fingers pumping slowly in and out, filling the room with the melody of my dripping core. I sigh with frustration as I continue, but pull back every time I get too close. When I start to get irritated, he senses it and smiles.

"You want to come, Killer?" he asks, taunting me with my own orgasm that I could take at any time, but I don't. I want his permission and I want to be told. I've never experienced true submissiveness, but if it's anything even remotely like this, it's exactly what I need. I nod my head desperately to his question.

"Yes," I pant in between breaths and thrusts of my fingers. "Please."

"I want you to crawl to me, but keep those fingers off the ground. Do you understand?" He questions my compliance. I'd do anything he wanted right now if it meant welcoming in the orgasm I've kept at bay at his request.

I release the stiff hold I had on my dress, and fight the urge to wipe off my fingers when I slowly pull them out of myself. Lowering to the ground on my knees and the heels of my palms, we lock eyes and he keeps stroking himself as I crawl to him. When I reach his feet, he moves his hand from the back of his head to under my chin, and the sensation makes me feel cherished and seen.

"Let me see those fingers, Killer," he says, and I hold up the two I had inside of me just moments ago. They're still glistening in the daylight streaming through the window, and I don't feel an ounce of shyness anymore. He looks at them and then to me with pride. "Put them in your mouth."

The command goes straight to my clit and I can feel my juices drip down my legs and onto the carpet. I don't lose the lock I have on his blue eyes as I part my lips and hollow my cheeks to suck every bit of myself off of my fingers just like he asked. His thumb strokes the side of my chin and I can feel his praise before I hear it. I only break eye contact when a drop of his arousal falls from the tip of his cock, and although I've never been a huge fan of giving head, my mouth waters at the idea of making him weak with every part of me.

"You want to taste it, don't you?" he asks when he catches me looking. I nod with sincerity, and he creases his dark brows trying to hold back. "Open your mouth and stick your tongue out, baby."

I do exactly as he instructs and his hand moves to the back of my head to grip my hair, pushing my open mouth over his weeping cock. The fingers I just cleaned from my arousal are already back to my clit working small circles, and I don't care if he told me to or not. As he uses the fistful of my copper locks to control the speed and depth of my mouth, I moan over him at the feeling of being stimulated in two places at once. When he catches my discretion, he knows I can't wait any longer and he pulls me off of his cock with a pop of my lips. Holding my hair back so I'm forced to look at him, he steels his expression so I know what he says next is not a suggestion or a question.

"Get the fuck up here and sit on my cock, Killer. Come on," he says as he helps me up. Lifting my dress, he pulls me onto his lap. When he lines himself up with my entrance, I suddenly know it won't be gentle, but I don't give a shit. I don't *want* it to be gentle. I feel like I'll explode if I have to hold back any longer and I don't want to make love. I want to be fucked. "Let me in that pretty pussy, baby. Put me in."

When I look down, I see he's holding my weight in his hands so I'm hovering over his lap. He wants me to choose. He's making me direct his cock inside me so I know this is real. Understanding my choice, I don't hesitate to wrap my fingers around him as we both watch and when I slip the head of him past my opening, I look at him.

"I want you, Clif. Do it. Fuck me," I say so there's not one small ounce of confusion as to what I'm consenting to and what I'm asking him for. He barely waits for me to finish speaking before he slams me down on his lap, releasing my full weight onto his cock. We both cry out and with the sunlight streaming in, there's no questioning it anymore; we're both into this and we're doing it because we want it. We fucking *need* it and we couldn't stop it if we tried.

He starts to move, and I wrap my arms around his neck while he grips the sides of my hips to control the motion of my body. The feeling of him filling me is intense, but the impending orgasm is otherworldly. I move myself faster and faster, and he pulls my dress over my head to let his eyes fall on more of my body. I almost don't feel my bra clasp, but the straps tug on my arms as he rips it off of me and throws it to the floor. For a second, I notice that I'm completely naked and he's still wearing all of his clothes, but before I can say anything, he moves his thumb to circle my clit. Without warning I erupt into the strongest orgasm I've ever felt in my life.

He slows his pace a little to let me ride it out, but it doesn't last long when I feel that he's almost there too. Drunk off the power I feel, I take both of his hands and hold them locked behind his head so he can't control anything anymore. The spark in his eyes flickers and he gyrates his hips upward into me. That's the last move I let him make before I hold his wrists tighter while I roll my hips harder and faster on him. When I'm almost there again, I look into his eyes and he stares as if he's in awe.

Before I can think of anything to say, I get a small one-pulse warning before my next orgasm crashes into me recklessly and without abandon. In my moment of disorientating ecstasy, he frees his arms from my hold, and with his hands cupping my breasts to his face, he comes with a roar right into my sternum.

We stay locked together for a few minutes while he drips out of me and wipes the sweat from his brow onto the sides of my breasts. When he finally looks at me, I see someone I've grown oddly fond of and have started to feel a deeper connection to. I pushed him away and he didn't run. He saw the absolute worst version of me and he helped me handle it. He might be shitty with money and debatably shittier at poker, but when it comes to me, I'm starting to trust him even though the logical part of me begs me not to.

"Let's get you cleaned up, Killer," he says with a smile. The voice he used to tell me to fuck my fingers is gone, and now he's softly making sure I'm ok. I don't protest as he carries me into the bathroom so I can pee while he starts the water for a bubble bath.

In an hour, I'm wearing a white hotel robe with wet hair that he shampooed for me while eating room service dinner. It's not even that much later that I'm talking to him one minute and the next, the world drifts into a peaceful dreamy darkness.

# CHAPTER SEVENTEEN

## Clif

I wake up to Sonnet buried in my chest, sound asleep. Looking at her cradled into me, I promise myself that I'll find a way, a legal way, to pay her back for the money I had to steal from her mother. Even if shit was rough with her mom, I still fucking hate the idea that I caused her more grief. Why wasn't it anyone else at that gas station and not her? I was only in that house for less than an hour, but if that bedroom was any indicator of what life with Gloria Franklin had been like, I can't imagine how Sonnet did it for so long. No wonder the girl loved fantasy romance books. It was probably her only escape, and from the looks of what must have been her father's book collection, maybe her dad wanted out too.

Trying my best not to wake her, I pull out my phone and text Walt that I'm on my way with merchandise to pay off my loan a little early. I almost waited, but after they surprised us at the last spot and fucked with Sonnet, I don't want to give anyone time to think about coming near her again. When I get the approval for a meeting from Walt, I pay for an Uber to take me. I don't want to take one more damn thing from her, so I'll use the small amount of cash I have to get to the drop, and then shamelessly beg them for my fucking wheels back. Once I pay, they'll have no reason to hold them anyway. That was the deal.

Leaving a note for her on the nightstand, I take a moment to wish that I'm not gone long enough for her to need to read it. It's not a goodbye, it's just a be right back, but I fucking hate writing about what I'm going to do because it's a reminder to her of what I am. Getting the notification that my ride is outside, I look at her one more time before slipping out of the room as quietly as possible.

When I'm dropped off at the location Walt sent me, I look around the abandoned gas station for any signs of life, but there's no one here. I pull out my phone, but before I can do anything other than unlock it with my face, a black Suburban pulls in next to me with my stolen BMW right behind it. I hold onto the hope that if my car is here, it means that I'll be leaving in it. I watch Walt get out of the Suburban with two cronies while the fuckface ogre that threatened Sonnet gets out of my car.

With us all standing next to pump three, I pull the rings out of my pocket and hand them to one of the bearded guys next to Walt. When I open my mouth to speak, Walt holds up a hand as a warning, I'm sure, not to say anything yet until the jewelry is examined for authenticity and cleared as a debt payment.

"Value for these three, boss, you're lookin' at twelve stacks," the man announces. Walt looks at me with a raised eyebrow.

"I owe you ten, but I'm putting in twelve for a show of good faith...and to get my ride," I answer.

Walt eyes me for a moment before nodding his head at the brick wall of a man I'd like to punish for touching my girl. *My girl. Mine.* Shit. I almost miss the keys being tossed at me a little harder than necessary, but the ownership settles in my bones. She belongs to me now.

"TJ tells me you have a little bird with you," Walt says with amusement and I shoot that big formerly nameless asshole a sharp glare. "So she *is* yours, isn't she? Heard she was a pretty one...TJ here says she smells like strawberries."

"Are we done here? We're square," I say, shuffling over to my car, but TJ approaches and crosses his arms in front of him. I'm being blocked in and for whatever reason, they're not done with me.

"You know I almost didn't believe him when he told me about her, but then there she was right on the tv. She just lost dear old Mom. Must be so alone now, poor bird. Good thing she's got a guy in debt to help her watch over that money when she's home alone," Walt taunts.

"What's your point? And I'm not in debt as of 30 seconds ago." I clarify impatiently. I'm not catching the point of this shit, but it fucking stinks already. If we were straight, our business should be done, and I should be back on the road in my own whip on the way to crawl back into bed with my Little Killer. I look at Walt and then to the other guys, and they all share a sickening grin, like they're waiting for me to figure out a joke at my expense.

"My point is, TJ reported back that Strawberry lives on Revello Circle. That's a *real* nice block of town. Real ritzy like. Then you come back here early with a handful of her mama's jewelry, and I think to myself...smells like there's more where that came from," he says as my stomach sinks. "I'm thinking it smells like a new deal."

"No fucking way, I'm not stealing from her. I'm paid, I'm fucking out. I'm going straight with her," I explain with my hands up in surrender. Whatever cut they would offer me isn't worth it. I won't do that to her. I can't. The guys all laugh and whatever is so funny, I have a feeling I won't be fucking laughing.

"We know you've gone soft, Clif, you never had that alligator blood in you. All you have to do is keep quiet, keep her out of the house tonight, and we'll be even. One night and you're off our radar for good... so is she and so is Little Joey," Walt offers. There it is. As soon as he lays it on the table, my fucking heart fills with lead and sinks to the bottom of my shoes.

"And if I refuse?" I ask quietly, already sensing the response and bracing for the blow.

"You think you can say no to me, kid? I'm going to that house tonight whether you're there with her or not...TJ didn't even want me to warn you, but what can I say? I'm a nice guy. He wanted her there sleeping naked in the dark, but I'm giving you the privilege of keeping her away. And Joey? You know it ages you in the pen when you're always worried about who's around every corner and what they want from you. I could make him untouchable," Walt finishes, and I hear the pounding of my heart. "Come on, aren't you tired of worrying about the kid?"

I understand now why they laughed. They're watching me come to the realization there's no fucking way out of this. There's no way I can tell Sonnet and there's no way I can protect her or Joey aside from just keeping her away. This will crush her, but the fucking alternative is standing there with yellow teeth waiting for an excuse to touch her. I straighten my spine and clarify the shitty deal I'm being pushed into. Might as well fine-tooth comb this shit because it's all I have left to do to feel any semblance of control.

"So I keep her out of the house tonight, you clean it out, and then you and fucking Shrek over here keep all hands off my girl and my brother for good?" I ask. There's a pause and TJ's eyes narrow at me, but I can't bring myself to give a single solitary fuck about it anymore.

"All hands, all mouths, all dicks away from them both. They're off limits for good. You hear that...Shrek?" Walt chuckles at the name and so do the other guys. TJ however growls and glares at me like he'd like to bash my brains in. "Here's a gift for your cooperation, or as you said 'a show of good faith'."

Walt walks close enough to me that I can smell the whiskey on his breath and the cigar smoke off his clothes. I bet I could even hear the cards shuffle and the chips stack if I closed my eyes. He holds out Sonnet's stolen driver's license with a few hundreds to me that he slips from his billfold, and I look at him curiously.

"Take your Little Strawberry out for dinner. She just lost her mother and I'm sure she could use a relaxing night out. Dinner, drinks...dick," he laughs as he uses his other hand to tap my crotch with his knuckles. I flinch and they all erupt in laughter. I take the money and it makes me feel sick, but if I have to do this one last thing to protect them both, then I don't see what other choice I have. The alternative destroys them both. What's property crime against what they could do to Joey or what TJ wants with Sonnet. There's no choice. I won't put them in danger.

"We'll text you a signal when it's over," Walt says as they all pile into the black Suburban, leaving me with my car. Before Walt closes his door, he turns to me. "If anything goes wrong tonight, Clifton, I'm certain you'll never forgive yourself for the payments I'll have to collect. Capisce?"

I gulp and nod, unable to form words at the horrifying imagery forced into my mind. Walt closes his door and they drive off, leaving me there in a cloud of desert dust. Turning to the side, I empty my stomach of the room service breakfast and try to catch my breath.

# CHAPTER EIGHTEEN

## Sonnet

When I woke up to Clif's note on the nightstand, I actually smiled. I can't remember the last guy who wrote me a note that wasn't my dad, especially if you don't count cards for birthdays or anything. Seeing his handwriting is like watching him when he's not looking. I don't know what we're doing or what we are, but I'm not in my usual hurry to label things or put them in a box. I do, however, strangely consider him mine through serendipity, fate, or trauma bonding. He feels like he belongs to me, like we're in this together now. We're a team.

By the time I'm showered and wearing another dress I packed from home, I hear the lock click on the door. With my last swipe of mascara he walks in, and as I turn to greet him with a warm smile, it immediately starts to fall when I see his face. He doesn't slow his stride as he walks right up to me, lifting me to stand next to him so he can wrap me in a hug.

"Umm, hey. You ok?" I ask, uneasy with the shift in his mood. He pulls back, holding my face in his hands to bring me in for a soft kiss with closed lips. He seems desperate, but for what I'm not sure as his eyes go back and forth between mine seeking solace.

"Just...I saw that guy that threatened you and it pissed me off. I'm done with them now and I got my car. I just...I..." he stutters. Putting my hands on top of his, I brace him to my cheeks and turn my head slightly to lay a light kiss on his palm.

"You can tell me. You can tell me anything, Clif," I say into his hand before turning my head back to face him. His ocean eyes flow into the earth of mine and he sighs, trying to find the words.

"What we've done; what we've been through...when TJ held you, I was scared and I was pissed. I wanted to kill him. I wanted to put a bullet in his skull because I realized something," he says as kisses my forehead. "I want to keep you, Killer. I wanted him dead because you're mine and he tried to hurt you."

His look changes from adoration to possession as he puts into words the magnetism between us. "Y-you want me to belong to you?" I ask in a whisper with my brows drawn. "Why?"

"...You didn't run..." he mouths and I almost miss the words. When I tell him I'm confused without putting voice behind it, he pets my hair. "When shit with Joey got fucked up and the cops came, he told me to run and I did. I thought he was right behind me, but even when a small part of me doubted he was, I still...I fucking ran...from what I can tell, your mom was a fucking bitch, but when she got sick, you were there. When she almost fucking killed you, Sonnet, you saved yourself. When I hurt you...you fought me. Shit, even when TJ had a gun to your head, you almost broke his fucking nose...and when I said crawl...you fucking loved it. How could I not want to keep you all to myself?"

"I think…I want to be yours," I admit to myself and out loud to him too. He pulls me in for a hug and rocks us back and forth. "What do we do now?" I ask with a chuckle into his shirt.

"Let me take you out on a first date tonight," he offers, speaking the words into the top of my head as he rests his chin there.

"I was going to clean out some stuff from the house tonight because the funeral home called, and I pick up her ashes tomorrow. I kind of want to get back to normal, you know?" I explain, hoping he doesn't think I mean normal as in pre-Clif. "You can come with me."

"Give me one more night here. Let me take you out to dinner, then we come back here and we can do anything you want, Killer," he borderline begs, and it's melting me that he's being so sweet. I pretend like I'm seriously contemplating, but I don't mind one more day with him, especially if we can act like a normal new couple for a while. "Then tomorrow, we'll handle the tough shit, and I'll be there for however much you want me to."

"Ok fine, you win. It's date night," I laugh as he picks me up to spin me in a circle. He kisses the top of my head again, making me almost forget that we've been held at gunpoint and covered up a murder in the past few days. I'm just going to let myself enjoy this little fantasy for as long as I can. Maybe it will just bleed into normalcy. "No pressure."

"I picked up some clothes from my place on the way, so let me shower and change first. Then we're going…I don't know, wherever you want, and we can do all the usual first date things," he says as he grabs a bookbag and heads to the bathroom.

"Yay! Terrible stories of our exes with questions about politics, religion, and kids," I call out playfully. I hear him chuckle as the bathroom door shuts and the shower starts.

While I wait, since I have a little time to kill, I call work to let them know I'll be ready for return after my full bereavement allowance expires in three more days, and then set a time with the funeral home for pickup tomorrow. As I scroll through the countless messages and notifications of everyone's deepest sympathies, they all seem so generic and mindless that they begin to blend together. It feels like a weighted blanket over me when I'm already too warm, and I start mass deleting them without even reading or responding. All I want to do is move on and start living my life the way that I want to live it without the nagging disapproval she sprinkled over everything and everyone I tried to love. I just want to blink and skip this part.

I'm going to clear out what I want from that house and estate sale the rest, leaving whatever doesn't sell to the shelters. The only things that mean anything to me are in that house, but once I remove them, I'll be able to love them in the open at a new place that's just mine. I want a fresh start for my life and to experience waking up without wishing I was easier to love. I didn't realize how caged I was until I saw everyone else flying by outside the bars, but now that I can, I'm going to soar. I send an email to a realtor I met through a mutual friend and let them know I'd like to sell the house, citing bad memories and the like before rotating through my brain rotting apps to take my mind off of everything.

When Clif finally comes out of the bathroom, he's in a gray button up shirt and black trousers with a clean shaven face and his hair finger combed out of his eyes. He looks...delicious. I offer to change, but he swoops me into his arms and shakes his head as he kisses me deeply. We leave the hotel and he pulls my hand as I walk toward my car to steer me another way. Seeing the BMW at the end of the lot, I know it's his. You know how they say dogs look like their owners? Well, this sleek sexy car looks exactly like Clif.

He opens my door for me and I don't think I've ever experienced that in real life from anyone that wasn't my dad. The more I think about it, the more irritated it makes me. Everyone I've dated had connections to my mother and her friends, as they tried to set me up with someone of their own standards. Every one of those men turned out to be nothing I wanted. As I watch Clif back out of the parking space with his arm behind my headrest, I can't help but drool over his sleeves rolled up to expose his patchwork tattoos. I smile to myself thinking about how much my mother would have hated that.

When we pull up to Antonio's, I'm already anxious that I'm underdressed. As I start to fidget, he puts a hand on my thigh to ground me and I smile. He's seen me unhinged, but I'm nervous he might not like me on a date or in the monotonous routine of regular life. It's like a relationship going in reverse, but for some reason, it works for us. With a wordless soft kiss on my closed lips, he jogs to my side of the car to open my door, and leads me inside where I'm surprised to find we already have reservations.

As our first glass of wine is poured, one that we chose at random, the server brings a basket of bread before leaving us to peruse the menu that doesn't even have the prices listed. I've been on dates where the guy just wants to show off, but this is different. Clif is different, and I guess I'm different from the girl that went on those dates too.

"Lay it on me, Killer. Tough first date question time," he jokes, setting aside his menu when he's decided on an entree. I lay mine down on top of his and make an exaggerated thinking face. "Anything."

"Hmm...ok let's start easy. What's your family like?" I ask, taking a sip of my wine and picking apart a piece of bread. He does the same and lays his life out like an open book.

"My mom skipped out on us because dad wouldn't change. He was in and out of prison until he died. All I had left was Joey. With his brains and potential, I just always assumed he'd go big and leave everything about this town behind. He always found a reason not to leave.

He went to community college closeby when he could have probably gone to some fancy big school. He got a steady job in accounting, but he could have been more if he wasn't worried about leaving me. When he got busted because of me, it fucked me up. I'm saving up to hire a lawyer though because Joey's free legal was a piece of shit, and the evidence the court had shouldn't have been enough to convict him. I don't know how, but know he's in there because fucking Walt wants my balls on a leash," he coughs on his bread when the server returns and almost hears the last line. We order our dinner and when we're alone again, we pick up where we left off, adding more wine to our glasses. "You want kids?"

"Wow, ok, my turn in the hot seat," I laugh. "No, I don't. You?"

"Nope. I don't want to bring a kid into my shit, plus this world is too fucked up anyway. I'd be too scared. I couldn't even keep Joey safe and I almost lost you..." he trails off, looking at me in the ambient lighting of the restaurant. He looks like a fallen angel, tortured and beautiful. A tragic hero with the best of intentions.

"Well, you didn't. Do you, umm, how do you vote?" I ask, which has been a deal breaker for me in the past, especially with a mother that hated everyone that wasn't her standard of natural pageant perfection. "Because that's important even if we don't want kids," I say, catching my slip. I see it his eyes that he heard it too.

"*We*," he repeats with a gorgeously mischievous smile. "I don't care what anyone else does with their body or their life as long as they don't get in the way of other people doing the same. Do your thing, but let me do mine and we all fuck off and leave each other alone," he finishes with a shrug. "I don't know what they call that, but I think everyone deserves to be happy as they are."

"You passed."

"Whew, I was fucking scared for a minute, Killer," he laughs openly and it pulls my giggle out too. "What will you do now that you're free from your prison, Dragon Princess?" he asks as he reaches over the small table to tuck my hair behind my ear. I melt right over my chicken piccata and blush, hoping he can't see it in the dim lighting.

"I...I don't know. I emailed the realtor today to tell her I want to sell the house. I guess I'll have to think about where I want to be now that I can do whatever I want," I shrug, not knowing how to reassure him that wherever I go, I want him with me if he wants to be. It seems scary to admit so soon, so I just let it linger.

"Where would you go if nothing mattered? When you dream of paradise on earth, where do you go?" he wonders out loud, and I can't wait to turn this question back around on him. But I close my eyes to pull the image I've slowly built more detail into as I've grown up.

"It's not the desert or the beach. When I think of paradise, it's full of trees and rain with a small lake. I'd choose a modern cabin with big windows and a fire pit out back. I'd have big rescue dogs and a room like my dad's full of bookshelves and all the fantasy stories I want...and I'd open the windows just to hear the rain like music," I say with a sigh. Sometimes when I think about that place, I can smell the pine and hear the rain falling onto nature like percussion instruments.

"That sounds like paradise to me," he matches my sigh and rests his chin on his palm. I smile seeing his elbow on the table, and although my mother would have hated that, I mirror his movements. "Could I have a bookshelf for my books too?"

"Hmmm, we'll see," I act like I'm giving it serious thought. "Depends, do you like dogs or cats?"

"I feel like this is a bear trap question, but my honest answer is both," he laughs as I narrow my eyes with skepticism. "I'm serious, Killer. I love both. We had a German Shepherd growing up named

Cora, but then Joey would always take me with him to sneak food to the stray cats in the neighborhood. He even let me name a few of the regulars."

We spend hours at the table with me finishing off the whole bottle of red, and asking each other everything we could think of that we'd ask on a first date. From embarrassing moments to go-to karaoke songs to our undying loyalty to House Targaryen, it felt like everything I hoped dating would be before my mother's matchmaking ruined it all.

When he pays the tab, we stand up and I waver a little on my feet. Putting a hand to my forehead, I hide the embarrassment seeping out of my pores just like the smell of the cabernet that I can't even pronounce anymore because my tongue feels huge in my mouth.

I feel the wind on my face and through my hair as we ride in his car with the windows down.

I feel the fluffy bed and the sheets around me like clouds.

I close my eyes and I'm in the cabin listening to the rain while I read to him on the couch, and then it's dark.

# Chapter Nineteen

## Clif

I wake up to the sunlight shining through the blinds I forgot to close as it streams around Sonnet, illuminating her hair like a little Greek goddess. I hated lying to her last night, but the time we spent together was so different from anyone else I've ever been around. She's funny, smart, and her imagination is full of make believe worlds I want to visit with her. Once she kept downing the wine, I didn't know when to stop her since I had no idea what her tolerance was. Turns out, it's probably around one and a half glasses, not five. I hadn't planned on sleeping with her, but her passing out made it a lot easier than me trying to explain why I wasn't pawing at her like I wanted to. It just didn't feel right.

When the alarm on her phone goes off, she jumps and immediately holds her head as she reaches for it. Taking a moment to let the disorientation fade, she looks down to see she's still wearing her dress from dinner, and she's wrapped in the blankets and in my arms. She smiles up at me and squints from the light, which is probably less enjoyable to her than it is for me.

"Oh my god, I'm so sorry I ruined our first date," she whines, pulling the blankets over her head and cuddling into my bare chest. I pull the sheets off of her messy copper hair and smile at her. How could I be upset with her? She has no idea what waits for her, and I want her to cherish whatever peace she can find before she opens the door to her mother's house. I'll fucking hate Walt forever for making me do this to her. Luckily, she'll never have to know I knew.

"Nah, cheer up, Killer. Without that liquid courage, I never would have heard your version of Britney Spears' greatest hits the entire way back here," I tell her only to watch her face melt into mortification. She's fucking adorable like this. Hard to believe everything else I know about her when she looks at me with those eyes.

She groans, putting her face back under the covers, and I can't help but wrap my arms around her. When her alarm rings again, it's from under the blankets, and she turns it off in less than a few seconds before letting out another growl. As she sits up, free of cover from the bed, I get a good look at her. She looks like she's more well-rested than before, and her stomach is growling even if she's a little bit hungover.

"I have to be at the funeral home in an hour," she says to me as she stretches her arms over her head, making her shoulders crack. "You really really...really don't have to come with me," she adds, giving me the out she thinks I might need, but I don't waver.

"I'm not going with you because I think I have to. I want to. I told you, I'm with you for all of it as long as you let me," I reassure her, putting my hand over hers. She drops her chin to break eye contact and flushes the sweetest fucking shade of pink. "Go on, you shower and I'll order us something to eat."

She flashes that stunner smile at me and hops out of bed to the bathroom. When the door shuts, I call down to the desk to order room service, and check my phone every five seconds for the "all clear" signal from Walt. It should have already happened, but who knows with his guys. They could rob a bank in the busiest hour of the day in plain sight and somehow still get away with it for how many people he has on his fucking payroll. When she comes out of the bathroom in jeans and a dragon t-shirt, I'm amazed at how beautiful she is even at her most casual.

With both of us dressed and breakfast finished, she's a lot more alert with an iced coffee in her. I let her drive today since she hasn't told me yet where she wants to spread her mother's ashes. If I had to guess how many times I've anxiously checked my phone to see if there's any news, I'd say it's been at least every minute. I just need it in writing that she and my brother are safe for good, and then we can move on with our lives.

When we pull into the funeral home, I put my hand on the door handle, but she stops me.

"I'm leaving it running. I'll just be a minute. Is that ok?" she asks, making sure I'm not offended.

I've tried to reassure her all day that there's nothing she could ask me to help with that would be too much for me. I want her to know I can handle it all for her. I nod, and she's gone in a blur, so I check my phone again. When I see no new messages, I decide to say "fuck it" and message him.

**Me: Is it done? I want this over with.**

I wait for an immediate response, but I can't even see read receipts because Walt has a fucking flip phone. Typical for him, I guess. He's in his 70s and I'm stuck waiting on his stupid ass to text me back. When Sonnet gets back in the car, she holds a small box in her hands. She looks to me, and I open my palms face up to let her know it's ok to ask me to hold the box until we reach wherever we're going. I'm just fucking praying that it's not her house.

"Where are we going to...you know?" I ask with the box in my hands while she backs out of the parking space and heads down the road in the opposite direction. I watch her to see if I'm going to have to persuade her to avoid her house, but luckily I don't have to.

"We're going to my dad's gravesite. I think he was the only thing that ever made Mom happy," she shrugs as she drives, keeping her eyes on the road, and her hands firmly gripping the wheel. "I'm going to leave her with him."

"That sounds kind of you," I offer, not knowing what else to say and watching her carefully for signs of breakage around the edges of her resolve. She nods her head, but doesn't speak another word. I'm relieved we're buying Walt and his guys more time in case they still haven't finished the job, but I fucking hate the longer this drags on. I am being honest about her being kind about leaving her mother's ashes near her father. We both know Gloria Franklin doesn't deserve this mercy, but even after everything, Sonnet still grants her peace.

She doesn't speak until we pull into the cemetery and ride along the paved way that circles the stones. Putting the car in park and taking the box from my lap, she doesn't utter one word as she gets out to walk a determined path toward a small stone near the iron fencing. I know she didn't tell me whether to stay or follow, but without knowing what emotions war within her, I exit the car and stay a close distance behind her. When we reach the stone, she kneels and touches her fingertips to her lips to kiss them before resting them on the small gray slab that reads Phillip R. Franklin.

"Hi Dad," Sonnet whispers to the stone. I slowly reach her and kneel next to her. "This is Clifton, Dad. He helped me with Mom."

When she looks at me with a soft close-lipped smile, I nod not knowing what's appropriate or acceptable to do in this situation.

"It's umm nice to...hi, sir," I stutter and she reaches over to squeeze my hand. Watching her reaction to the death of her mother versus visiting the grave of her father, it's not at all hard to see who made her feel loved.

"Dad...I brought Mom to you. She didn't want a burial, but the only time she was ever happy was with you, so...I'm going to leave her where she'd want to be," she says quietly. Removing her trembling hand from mine, she opens the small white box. When she reaches the bag within, she's shaking so much that she can't open it easily. With a pleading look to me, I understand.

"I got it, baby, it's ok," I whisper to her as she nods and thanks me with her eyes. I open the bag effortlessly and we hold it together as we spread the ashes around the area of where her father's coffin lies below. When the bag is empty, I close the box and hold it under my arm while I remain quiet and motionless, allowing her to set the pace. If she wants to sit here for an hour, we sit here for a fucking hour. Whatever she needs, I'll give it to her.

After a few minutes longer, I watch her wipe a tear discreetly as she takes a few deep breaths. When she slowly gets to her feet, I follow her motion and we walk to the car without another word. I put the small box in the backseat of the car, but I'm barely in my own seat before she reaches over the center console to pull me into a hug. I'm not even sure if a hug is the right word. She buries her face into my chest and fists my shirt in her hands while I wrap my arms protectively around her. Holding her there in silence, I rub her back and offer her the comfort she needs.

As her breathing levels, I feel my phone vibrate rapidly indicating the three incoming texts, and I dread what I'll see when I get the chance to look. When she pulls back from my chest, she nods and wipes the wetness from her cheeks before she buckles her seatbelt to put the car in drive.

"Thank you for doing that with me, Clif. You didn't have-" she starts.

"Don't thank me. I wanted to be there for you and I'm here for as long as you want me to be," I reassure her again as she drives along the pathway to the exit of the cemetery. "What do you want to do now?"

Before she answers, I slip my phone out of my pocket and hold it discreetly next to my leg as I read the messages I received. Sure enough, it's fucking Walt and the fucking shit storm he's got me stuck in.

*Walt: All square, boy.*

*Walt: We're done here. Your bird and your brother are off limits.*

*Walt: Come see me when you want in on another game. I'll keep your seat warm at the table.*

"Maybe start going through the house? I want to make sure it's ready for the realtor, so there's some things I need to take care of before I go back to work. There's only a few things in that house that mean anything to me," she trails off, but I can't focus. Who knows what Walt and his guys did to her fucking house. I'm guessing they snuck in, grabbed the things that they found valuable, and Sonnet might not even know they were missing. He doesn't seem like the type to steal the tvs or anything like that. They were looking for the diamonds.

The only thing I know for sure is that even though I have to live with this lie in silence, it's worth it to know she's safe and so is Joey.

# CHAPTER TWENTY

## Sonnet

After exiting the drive thru, Clif and I decide to eat our double-doubles and fries on the way to the house. Every time I reassure him he doesn't need to do any of this with me, he reminds me that he wants to be here as long as I want him to be. I know I'm probably riding the line between clingy and standoffish, but it's only because I don't have the courage yet to tell him never to leave. It's not something I've ever felt or knew I needed, but I like having a partner in this. I don't know how I would have survived this ordeal without one if I'm being honest with myself.

When we pull into my driveway, I can already see the cards and flowers piled up on the front porch, and I'm caught off guard. It's still strange to me that the version of her I knew was only reserved for me. To the rest of the world, Gloria Franklin was a beautiful, but modest and humble gem who straightened the literal and figurative crowns of other women. I wonder if she ever looked at me the way others looked at her, with a warm admiration that whispered "she's just *so* sweet". Getting out of the car to approach the porch full of sympathy mementos for a woman I'll never know, Kathy's curtains shift next door before she steps outside to call out to me.

"I'm so sorry about your mother, honey. Do you need me to come over and help you with anything? I could make you and your...friend here something to eat," she calls out with a hand over her heart, her pink nail polish standing out against the white of her linen dress. Her eyes reach Clif with curiosity at first, but the longer we remain on the porch amongst the memorial gifts, she squints with scrutiny.

"No, um, thank you so much. This is my, well...," I stumble over my words to label him, but we haven't had that full discussion quite yet. "Clif is my friend and he's going to help me clean the house out for the realtor. I think it's time I look for a place of my own."

"That's probably best. It's a sad time, sweetie, but it would be so nice for you to find your own way and settle down. I know your momma just wanted you to have your own family one day," Kathy answers back with a sympathetic expression. Clif fidgets next to me uncomfortably and I sense he's a little on edge. Sure, over dinner we talked about kids and the future, but that was a silly wine-infused date for two people that are in a situation that's anything other than casual. He said it didn't scare him off, but I wouldn't blame him if it did.

Waving over at Kathy, I nudge Clif and he looks up from his phone that he's been hiding in and joins me in bidding farewell to the nosy neighbor. When I put the key into the lock, I grab his sleeve and pull him in with me to save him from the awkwardness of the interaction. He hesitates for a moment like he's second guessing if he should come in, but it's only a split second before he's inside with me and we're shutting the door to the outside world.

Pushing his back against the door to shut it the whole way, I run my hands up his chest and settle them around his neck. With my fingers in his hair and his hands settling on my hips to ground me in place, I feel a slight rigidity to his body. Leaning back a little to read what he's not saying in his blue eyes, I find they're not even on me at all. When I look at him, his attention is behind me. I turn instantly fearing what could create that reaction from him, but there's nothing there.

And that's when I see it. The shards of glass on the kitchen floor catch the sunlight through the window. The frames on the wall slightly at a slant like someone brushed by them in a hurry. The key dish next to the front door on the table is empty with its contents next to it having been dumped out as if someone was looking for something. For someone that has only been here once before, he's a lot more observant than I am. I freeze for a moment taking in the little details and I wonder if I should call the police before I touch anything. I pat my sides and remember I don't have pockets, so my phone is in the car.

"Shit, I have to call this in. Can I use your phone?" I ask Clif with an exhausted sigh. Just when I think this can't get any more disastrous, the universe gives me one more thing to tie me to this house and my mother. He pauses.

"Should we look around first to see what they took?" he asks, keeping his phone concealed in his hand at his side. I know it shouldn't bother me, especially because I didn't ask him if there was anyone else, but I can't help the small twitch in my eye and in my gut telling me something seems off. Shrugging that thought off until later, I step away from him to take a closer scan of the living room and kitchen area.

The garage door is closed. The glass on the kitchen floor looks like it's from the now gaping hole in the small window pane above the handle of the back door. That proves someone broke in, but for what? The tv is still mounted on the wall and when I open the garage door, the red Mustang is still there along with the keys. Clif is close behind me in the kitchen, his phone up like he's taking pictures of the damage.

I only wear the puzzled look for a minute before my attention goes to the stairs, and I'm past Clif and at the top in record time. Mom's door at the end of the hall is open and just from the doorway, I know where the intruders focused their energy. From the rectangle view of her room that I can see from my vantage point, there are clothes and belongings strewn across the floor and bed in a room that has probably never seen disorder.

In my mind, I think I'm running to her room, but in reality I move like I'm underwater with the shock setting in from everything I've endured in the past week. Clif doesn't say anything, he just puts a hand on my lower back as we walk, not to guide me, but to let me know he hasn't left me. Stumbling on the overturned corner of the runner, I reach out to the doorframe of my father's office to regain my balance, but when I take in what's in front of my eyes, everything stops.

"Hey, I got you," Clif starts as he stumbles with me, his phone falling out of his hands and bouncing off of the floor amidst the room that used to be my dad's office. "What the fuck."

I can hear him swear as he holds my shoulders, but it's like I'm in and out of my body at the same time. I struggle to slow my breath and my knees give out as I desperately try to process all five stages of grief one after the other in seconds. I open my mouth, but I can't find the words to speak or to scream. Everything that mattered to me feels like it was just ripped from the softest, most breakable part of my heart.

"I-I-they...his desk," I manage to whisper through hyperventilating. Clif holds me to his chest as we sit on the floor rocking back and forth. With one hand on the crown of my head, the other rubs my back in up and down motions until I start to feel my heart rate slow.

It's then that the anguish leaves my body. The tears I didn't know how to have for my mother are flowing out of me in spades when I experience the loss of my father for what feels like the second time in my life. That room had been an unspoken shrine that as much as Mom and I didn't agree on anything else, we both respected the need to maintain that space. It's not that we expected him to return by some miracle, but it was the only thing left between us that wasn't disappointment and resentment. Wrapped in Clif's warmth, I turn my head to look closer at the mess from the safety of his arms.

I don't know what the burglar was looking for, but it was common sense that they didn't need to empty every shelf of its organized collections of fantastical stories. Although some of the books had been first editions, signed special print runs, and beloved hand-me-downs from his parents, the floor is the great equalizer. Some covers had been ripped off and the framed maps he'd drawn from some of his favorite series were either tilted on their place on the wall or thrown to the ground. As defeating as that was, it wasn't what made me mourn what was left of his place in my soul.

The two drawers from the side of Dad's desk had been pulled from their tracks and lay empty on the floor with what was left of the contents strewn around the room. The photo of us that used to sit on top was smashed, and thrown into the trash bin in what seemed like the cruelest decision. Feeling the crippling fear of what I hoped not to find, I crawled off of Clif's lap over to the small drawer under where the keyboard would sit. Lifting myself up onto my knees, my hands felt like I was on pins and needles as I pulled the drawer open to look inside. Empty.

"No," I whispered, not even bothering to look at what was stolen from my mother's room. I didn't care. There were only a few things in this house that meant anything to me and none of them were in her room. They could have stolen the Mustang and I wouldn't have felt that torn up about it save for the loss of money and the fact that I'd have to interact with the police again.

"What is it, baby?" Clif asks in a breath, bringing my face up to level my eyes with his. His brows are furrowed and his eyes are bouncing to mine back and forth as if he's trying to read my mind through them. "Tell me what's wrong."

"Dad had a watch that he always kept in the drawer. It stopped working a long time ago, but it was the first thing he ever bought himself when he sold one of his maps to an author for their series. He bought Mom the car, and then the watch. He took it to the jeweler to engrave it for me. When the battery died, I realized he never wore it for the time. He just wanted part of me to be with him when he was on the road," I explain, barely finishing before the tears find their way down my cheeks again.

"I didn't know-," he says as he wipes my tears, and I see him start to stumble over his words. "-I mean, I bet they were just looking for stuff, you know?"

He settles back from me, patting his pockets and I sniffle. Running my hands through my hair, I cough and brace myself as we both help each other to stand. Leaning against the desk, I look over at him with narrowing eyes as I watch him focus on everything but me. I don't know why I feel like he's not in here with me even though he is, but what they say about women's intuition isn't a joke.

"Clif, can you get me a glass of water? Please?" I say between coughs and he regains his focus on me to assess my stability. "I'm ok, I just feel dry in my throat."

With a nod and a kiss to my forehead, he rushes out of the room and I hear his heavy footfalls down the stairs. I know it was shitty to pretend I needed something, but I had to buy a minute of time without him watching me. Looking at the corner of the room, I spot where his phone had landed next to a pile of what used to be a George R. R. Martin collection. As a girlfriend, or even a daughter, I'd never snooped through someone else's phone, but there was something nagging in my gut, and if I was wrong, I could always just say it rang.

Rushing over, I pick up the phone and instantly rejoice at the fact that it wasn't locked with his face or a passcode. It must have been unlocked when it hit the ground. With a single swipe, I'm on edge as I tap the little envelope icon. The messages I start to read confirm something worse than I could have expected. While I was worried about another woman, he was lying to me about something else. Hearing his footsteps stop in the doorway, I look up at him. Wearing defeat and surprise on his face, his gaze falls to the phone in my hands...right before I launch it directly at his lying face.

# Chapter Twenty-One

## Clif

Not only do I drop the glass for it to shatter on the floor, splashing tap water everywhere, but I duck before my phone flies an inch away from my head and dents the wall to my side. Shit. She is fucking deadly. And then I remember she actually *is* fucking deadly. When Sonnet stands with a slight wobble, I put my hands out in surrender and to try to calm her down just long enough for her to understand why I had to do what I did.

"Sonnet, wait. Stop. I can explain, ok? Please. Fuck, let me explain," I say in panic as the words stumble out.

She takes three steady strides like she wants to sidestep me and escape the room that's now broken her heart twice tonight. I mirror her quickly, keeping my hands up while I block her path. The look she shoots me makes my body temperature rise, but not from arousal. I feel like her rage can touch me. Something about this room. I should have seen it before. I should have warned them. Trashing this room was personal. It reeked of TJ throwing a fit that Sonnet is off limits to him for good.

"Explain then, asshole," she spits with venom from her lips and daggers from her eyes.

"When I went to get my car, Walt and his guys, including the guy that grabbed you, said that they'd seen your address and they knew this part of town had money. I tried to tell them to fuck off, but they made me a deal, and-"

"-a deal?! Are you fucking serious? How much?" she shouts at me, waving her arms up in exasperation.

"What? No, you're missing it. It's not how much money, baby, it's your life and Joey's life," I try to explain, taking one experimental step closer to her. She doesn't move back, but I can see her body run stiff like she's bracing for pain or to run.

"So like you texted, you pretended to date me to keep me out of the house so they could take the one piece I had left of the only person that's ever loved me? Was fucking me a bonus too?" she asks while she shoves me hard in the chest with both of her hands, but she's too small to push me backward. I step into her, not willing to let her spiral into whatever this is.

"Fuck no. I didn't pretend to date you or fuck you for any reason other than if I didn't feel what it was like to be inside you, I'd die. I only swore to keep you out of this house for one night, and excuse me, but you drank yourself stupid anyway," I said too quickly and sprinkled it with instant remorse. I grab her upper arm to pull her into me and she looks at me like I'm a stranger.

"Why lie to me, Clif? You could have just told me what was happening! I could have slipped in quickly to grab the only things I care about in my entire life, in this entire house, and it wouldn't have mattered. Why?" she questions with a quivering lip that I'm sure is partly from sadness and the rest from the anger still lingering within her. Her eyes search mine for answers, and what I wouldn't fucking trade for some celestial power to grant me the foresight to give her the exact response that would make all of this stop and make her trust me again.

"I'm sorry, baby, I didn't know, I-"

"-you didn't even *try*," Sonnet speaks in a broken soft tone that fucking cracks me open with her.

"I was *trying* to keep you safe," I reply to her even though she didn't ask me anything. I tilt her chin up to me and I can see the exhaustion on her face that's physical and emotional. The light from the sun beginning to set makes her hair look like liquid fire and the tears that have begun to fall glow. She looks like a painting of a tragic goddess and I hate myself more with every second that passes. "They told me if I said a word, they would hurt you. The deal was to keep us both away from this house for one night, then you and Joey would be untouchable to them for good."

"So my father's memory bought my safety," she says with a nod as she explains it again out loud to herself. "And your brother will be safe in exchange now?"

I can see her process the position I was thrown into and why I did what I felt I had no choice but to do. There's nothing I can do to take back what I've done, but if given the chance to do it again, I don't see any other way to handle it. I might not be the best at navigating things like this or relationships, and I know that fucked me over, but I don't see the way out anymore. All I have left at this point is to tell the truth.

"Yeah. He's safe in there so I can just focus on the appeal," I start to explain and remember she's not exactly asking me because she cares about his well-being. She's never met him. She's trying to decide if the stolen memento of her father was worth it. I feel her body lose all tension and succumb to defeat. She takes a deep breath, and closes her eyes for a moment before opening them to level me with a resolve that doesn't look at all like the girl I went on a date with. Shit.

"I don't think I can forgive you for lying to me," she starts, avoiding eye contact with me so she can focus on the words she's trying to say. "And I can't replace what was taken from me because it's priceless, but I understand why you had no choice."

"Thank you, baby, I-" I start, but my relief is short lived as she cuts me off to finish doling out what feels like will be a punishment.

"-I know we're tied to each other for what happened, and we didn't trust each other right from the start. I did what I did too, and this is what I deserve for it. You don't have to pretend anymore, and we don't have to act like this is something that isn't just happening because of the situation. You had fun. I had fun. And that's what it was."

"Sonnet, look at me," I ask of her. I hold her tired upper arms and she tilts her chin up to meet my eyes. Blue to hazel. Ocean to earth. "I never lied to you about how I feel about you."

"You don't even know me, Jack. I was just the girl in the car. It could have been anyone and you'd be with them instead. It's just the situation," she answers with a shrug. It's like she's saying goodbye and I feel a sharp ache in my chest at the thought of her turning into a stranger. I don't want her to be right, but was it fate that put me in that car or desperation? I put my palm on her cheek, not knowing what to say, but trying my best to make it make sense to her.

"I don't care how I got to you, I'm here now. *We're* here now and nothing I said about us is a lie. I *do* want to be around as long as you'll have me and I like you a lot, Killer," I say with my thumb stroking small swipes across the streaks her countless tears had left. Just as I thought there was a look of vulnerability in her eyes, the warmth drained, and it was like I was just another patient in the ER on a regular full moon night. Like I was all business. I felt myself lose her before she had to say it, but I braced myself anyway. At least she didn't have anything else to lob at me.

# Chapter Twenty-Two

## Sonnet

Slipping from his hold, I backed up to run a hand down my dress, straightening it like I hadn't just fallen apart on the floor of my dead dad's office. Clif looks at me like I'm an unpredictable animal that's been spooked. I can't tell if he's afraid I'll hurt him or break his heart, but I don't see how that's possible when we haven't even been a thing for that long. My heart hurts and I'm so tired of everything. As much as I understand him, I just don't think I can continue acting like we ever should have trusted each other.

"I got an email and a call from my mother's lawyer about her will. I'm sure your friends took everything from this house, and you're welcome to look if you want, but I don't think they're the type to leave a payday behind. Dad's watch might not tick anymore, but it's still a gold Rolex," I explain. When I see that he's not exactly following, I continue without making eye contact. I just want to be able to get this out and move onto cleaning this house. Maybe then I can find a new place to live where there aren't gorgeous tattooed carjackers or slimy loan sharks. "When Mom's stuff is finished through probate court, I will give you enough to pay for the appeal."

"No, I can't," Clif starts, holding a hand out for mine, but I pull back and cross my arms in a subconscious way to protect myself.

"It's ok, I want to. Your brother didn't do anything wrong and he doesn't deserve to be caught up in all this. I can appreciate that and give him a piece of what you wanted to get for him to make it right," I say with a nod of my head. It's finished, that's the plan, but there's one catch I have to push myself to stick to, and he senses there's more.

"At what cost?" he throws my earlier question back to me and at the very least, it shows that he was listening.

"I want you to leave. We'll trade numbers and I'll let you know when it's done. You can stay at the hotel if you want since it's paid for another night, but I'm staying here and I don't want anything else from you, Clif," I answer without hiding the disappointment with a touch of resolution in my voice.

"Sonnet, wait, ok? Let's just talk about it. We can do this together," he starts and I watch his mind race as he tries to bargain away the irreparable breach of trust between us. "Look, let me call Walt and maybe I can get the watch back for you. I didn't know."

"Just stop. It's gone and so is anything I thought we started together. It was just a whirlwind situation anyway. We had fun and now we're paying the consequences for what we've done. Let's just call it while it's early and we're not invested. Just...I want you to go," I say with my hands moving to my hips as I stand my ground atop the rubble of my memories.

For a second, he looks like he's going to spend the night trying to convince me to change my mind and take it back, but he stops when he sees the change on my face. The comfort I had in his arms is gone, and all I can think about is how this house holds nothing for me anymore and neither does he. He opens his mouth to speak, but closes it and presses his lips to a straight line, nodding at the irrefutable finality of it.

"I'm sorry, Sonnet," he offers softly. He bends down to pick up the phone I impulsively torpedoed at his head, and slips it into his pocket. Turning to leave me in the room alone like I asked him to, he stops to meet my gaze one more time. "If you need anything, I'm here. I don't want your money. I'll figure it out. This is my shit, but please, don't think for one fucking second that I don't care about you."

He pauses for a small moment, maybe waiting for me to respond, but I don't. I can't. I nod my head to acknowledge his words, but there's nothing I have left to offer anyone else. As I watch him leave, I can't tell if the room got lighter or heavier without him in it. His footsteps are soft on the stairs and when I hear the front door shut, I take a moment to bid farewell to the memory of this room. It doesn't even feel like Dad's space anymore. It belongs to no one. It just feels empty.

Walking out of the room, I stand in my mother's doorway to peek in. The closet is open, dresser drawers pulled and tossed to the floor, and her jewelry box is gone. The satin-topped hangers she used to hang her wardrobe are pointed at various angles as the clothing rests on the floor and off the corners. It's almost like I'm a forensic analyst and I'm visualizing the creation of a crime scene with blood splatter. I can almost see how someone would have entered the space solely to create havoc, purposefully making the violation more shocking upon discovery. It was about more than just the money. They did this because they could, and as hurt as I am, I know there's no possible way Clif would have let this happen if he knew this was the intention.

I don't even know exactly where to start at this point, so I decide to stay in my mother's room and start pulling her clothes into piles. I'll donate it to the women's shelters and make sure the fancier items go to the local at-risk youth programs so maybe they can help girls who can't afford prom dresses. I turn the music up on my randomized playlist to let the beat drown out the exhaustion and pity I feel for myself. It's hard to stay focused on it with Lady Gaga's "Judas" blaring.

A few hours and a small pizza from the freezer later, I've gotten through my mother's entire room and the last bit of vodka she had left. Looking back at the vacant room behind me save for the furniture and the bags to donate, I feel a little sense of dizzy peace. It's a relief to know that a donation drop, an estate sale, and a realtor are the only roadblocks to me severing the link I have to her.

With that room complete, I change my playlist and decide to rip the bandaid off as I brace myself and enter Dad's destroyed office and library; the place I used to lay on the floor and listen to him read or watch him create fantasy realms with charcoal pencils. The vodka in my system warms my throat to distract me from the painful lump of sadness that's trying to claw its way up to escape. I've cried so much already and as much as I try not to, I lose the battle in the doorway. I'll donate what I can, save what matters, and recycle the rest of the fantasy worlds in the hundreds of pages on the floor.

Book by book, memory by memory, I form three piles from the destruction. I'm angry at myself. I hate my mother for not being here and for never being what I wished she could have been for me. As the recycle pile grows taller than the others, my heartbreak rattles the bars of my ribcage. *Why trash the books beyond salvage?* They're just books. Then I furrow my brows when I realize again, it was to hurt Clif by hurting me. To throw a tantrum that I was untouchable. And I grimace again.

From the torn shreds of Middle Earth to Narnia, I put the worlds into a trash bag for recycling and blow a piece of copper hair out of my face. Any alcohol I'd welcomed into my system has dwindled and all I have left is how tired I am. With no deadline for having the house cleaned out, I decided that I would go back to my room downstairs and hope it still felt like mine.

I don't know why I hadn't thought to check it until now, but I pick up my pace as I glide down the stairs, checking the front door lock on the way. When I reach my room, my saddest suspicions are confirmed and everything I own is strewn around the floor. What disgusts me is that my underwear drawer is open and I don't even want to know what's missing from there. I recoil from the idea that that ogre of an asshole from the motel might have a pair of my panties, but it's short-lived when I see the shoebox that used to be under my bed on the opposite side of the room - empty.

I twist my head back and forth, looking for a small glint of uneven gold paint to reassure me that my security blanket token was safe. I tiptoe around the room, or what's left of it, careful not to step on anything except the small glimpses of the carpet beneath peeking out. When I near my closet door, I bend down instantly and curl my fingers carefully around it. My crown. My crown from when I was a kid dreaming about a whimsical world other than my own where I was someone to be admired and loved. Someone who was brave. And now with the three pieces it was left in after no doubt being thrown at the wall, I have nothing left that mattered to me.

I hold the pieces to my chest, as if I could touch it to my broken heart, and crawl into bed under my covers and the clothing that had been thrown on top. I don't even care. I'm just so done. I'm tired, and right before I let the darkness of sleep and defeat take me under, I fight the thought that creeps in without warning or permission. *I wish Clif was here to hold me.*

# Chapter Twenty-Three

## Sonnet, 10 Years Old

*A*s soon as I get in the car, I sit up straight against the seat so I can purposely rub the back of my hair to mess it up. I know Mom worked hard on it, but I told her that I wanted to go to work with Dad instead of wearing this stupid pink dress and dancing on stage for weird people to decide if I should win a crown or not. I didn't even want that crown. It was wrong. It didn't look like any of the crowns in my books, and I know for a fact these crowns don't come with a kingdom.

Mom is mad at me again and I know she wants me to win, but no matter how hard I try, I can't help that I'm just not good at it. I don't feel comfortable when everyone is staring at me and I hate the song Mom picked for me to dance to. It's not even music we like. It's something she chose from when she was a girl, and it made her mad when I missed the step on the last pose.

"Sonnet, I don't think I need to tell you how important practice is. Did you even do the counting in your head like we learned?" Mom asked, sounding tired and angry at the same time. She pulled the car out of the parking lot quicker than usual, and slammed on the brakes when *another car darted out. When she glared at me in the rear view mirror, I realized I was frantically nodding my head and she couldn't hear my response.*

*"I'm sorry, Mom. I counted, I promise," I lied. I really had meant to count like we practiced, but as soon as the bright lights made it hard to see and I thought about how much I missed Dad, I forgot. I missed the final step, and I posed one beat past the ending of the song. When the lights moved out of my eyes, I could see nothing but the look on Mom's face.*

*"Well, that's less time you'll be spending in your father's office reading those silly stories and more time to practice your routine. We will not be embarrassed like this again, Sonnet Elizabeth," she says while she lights a skinny cigarette. She knows the smell makes me gag, but she smokes next to me anyway. I know she hates me.*

*When we get home, I take off my fancy dress and put it in the closet along with my tap shoes and tights. Even though it's a little past dinner, I put my pajamas on anyway. I lay on my bed and pull the Dragon Princess book out from under my pillow to read chapter seven when Mom bursts in. I barely get the chance to hide it before she comes in. If she would have seen me with it, she would have taken it. I know it. She's got the phone in her hand and as it rests against her ear, she sits on the edge of my bed, tapping my leg to give her more room.*

*"Yes, she's right here and can tell you how she wasted your hard-earned money today when she decided not to count her steps like we talked about," Mom tattled on me to Dad before pulling the phone from her ear. "Your father would like to talk to you," she says like she's excited about me disappointing my dad.*

*"...H-hi Daddy," I say just above a whisper while Mom walks out of the room.*

"Hi Little Princess, what happened?" My dad's voice doesn't sound mad at all. He sounds a little sad, but not at me - for me.

I explained my missed step and how sorry I was and how much I tried my best. I told him how I'll do better next time and that Mom said it would come out of our reading time. I spoke quickly and softly until I could hear Mom's footsteps coming back.

"Sweetheart, do you want to be in pageants? Tell me the truth," Dad asked. I hesitated, afraid to say the wrong answer or get in trouble for my honesty considering how much money and time Mom had put in. "It's ok, you can tell me," he insisted.

"...no," I said in a whisper as Mom swooped in and grabbed the phone from my fingers before I could even say goodbye. She got back on the phone with her nice voice and shut my door behind her. I pulled my book out to go back to chapter seven. I wasn't even tired at first, but I slipped under my covers as I listened to the muffled sounds of my mother arguing with my dad.

When I woke up, it was to the sound of the front door opening and closing, signifying one thing - Dad was home! I rushed upstairs before even brushing my teeth to propel myself into the arms of my father who caught me and lifted me into the biggest hug that made everything feel like it was ok.

"Sonnet, get to the bathroom and get ready for the day right now. You are a mess," Mom said coming around the corner of the kitchen. I put my chin down and nodded in obedience before rushing to the bathroom. I wanted to hear about all the places Dad saw and how many new people got to see his drawings. I wanted to see what he brought me.

When my teeth are brushed and my face is washed, I push the headband onto my hair and slip on the dress Mom laid out for me. I don't have to guess where Dad is. I run right to his office next to their bedroom and I jump into his lap as he sits at his desk. Mom doesn't let me go into *that room when he's not there, so the fact that not only do I get to spend time with Dad, but I get to look at all the books makes me happy. It's like having our own special library right at home. He said if I get good grades, then he'll give me a shelf of my own to start collecting books too just like he does.*

*"Geez, my little warrior, you're getting heavy!" he laughs at the impact of me jumping onto his lap. I look down at the desktop to see what he's working on only to find a small box.*

*"What's in there?" I ask curiously, reaching out to touch it and then pulling back to wait for his permission. He laughs, moving his glasses up his nose when it crinkles.*

*"You can look, but it's just something I bought to remind myself of the two most important people," he explains while I open the box. Inside there's a beautiful gold watch that shines like the buried treasure we read about in last month's book.*

*"But...it's just a watch," I state plainly. It's pretty, but I don't see how a watch could remind him of me and Mom. I don't see how anything could remind him of the two of us at the same time. We've always been so different.*

*"See, that's where you need to look closer," he says with a hint of mystery and challenge to try again. He nods at me and I take that as a cue that it's alright to lift it from the box.*

*Pulling the watch from its bed and pushing the small pillow out from underneath it. I inspect it in my hands. The face was gold. The number markers were little gold lines. There was a magnified square for the date. My brows drew together as I wondered what the answer to the riddle could be.*

*"Is it because it's gold?" I try, but he softly smiles and shakes his head. Taking the watch from my hands, he turns it slightly into the light of his desk lamp while he explains.*

*"I sold my map drawing and I think it'll be in a book now. The money from that, I bought myself this reminder. The watch itself is for me, so I remember to follow my dreams. The front of it has a small crown, see? That's for your mom, my beauty queen. And see this?" he asks as the light catches the back of the watch. On the flat behind the face, there's something etched on it. Engraved right into the gold.*

*"Dad, is that..."*

*"A little dragon for my little Dragon Princess," he said with a smile and a ruffle of my hair on the top of my head. Even though I want to tell him I'm too old for that, I don't. The look on his face when he sees how much I love the symbol that reminds him of me is so happy, I don't even care if my hair is a mess. "Now you're both with me everywhere I go."*

*When my eyes return to the watch, I touch the dragon symbol so I can feel the etched lines in the gold. It looks like something a king would wear if the fantasy books we loved took place today. It's like a crown you wear on your wrist. A royal symbol my father would always have and I would forever be a part of it. Just like magic.*

*Minutes later, Mom calls from downstairs to come get something to eat. As I hop down, I look up at Dad and he puts a finger over his lips to shush me while he speaks.*

*"I'm going to talk to Mom about you and those pageants, ok? Then tomorrow, we'll read book 2 of the series," he reassures me. I know she'll be mad, but I'm glad I can go back to reading and spending more time in Dad's library room. I hope I get to have times like this forever.*

# Chapter Twenty-Four

## Clif

I keep replaying what happened in my head and every time it loops, I imagine it going down differently. First, I'm beating the shit out of TJ and telling Walt to stay away from her. The next time I picture it, I'm flipping on them and turning informant for the cops so they can put us in some witness protection program or something. In another version, I'm just telling her the fucking truth and she gets the chance to hit her house before they do so she can get her dad's watch. Over and over, I think about it. In every dream scenario, I do something other than what I did-which was fucking nothing. And in every replay I imagine, it ends with her not giving me that disappointed look while telling me it all meant nothing.

Snapping out of it, I look at her house one more time before I start driving. I don't even think about if what I'm about to do will get me killed or worse, but I know I have to do it while there's still time. I head back to where it all started. Back to where I could have avoided the entire fucking situation I'm in. Before I lost myself for ruined Joey's life. Before I met her.

When I see the faded sign that indicates parking is in the back, I get a flashback of the last time I was here. Marrin's Pub is the one bar I've never walked through the front doors of. Anyone that comes to this bar is either looking for shit you can't buy from a regular dealer, a hitman, or an invitation-only high stakes table. Luckily for me, I was only ever in need of the latter. I didn't tell Walt I was coming back to his spot tonight or ever. I don't know if it was to avoid him saying "fuck no" or laughing at me that I can't stay away, but both options make me feel sick. I wouldn't be here if I didn't need to be, but it's the only thing I can think about.

When I deliver a series of 6 knocks 3 times on the door, it opens a few inches to hide a view of the activities inside. I recognize the body that blocks the doorway and at the same moment, he smiles a toothy grin with a flash of gold on the left side.

"Well lookie who it is. You been outta the weeds for barely a night, and now you want back in, son?" he asks and his voice elicits a visceral reaction. I can still feel the pain of his shoe in my ribs and his fist on my face the night he stole my keys.

"Missed you too, asshole. I need to talk to Walt," I tell him without pouring my black heart out on the pavement. I can smell the cigar smoke from where I stand, and the sound of shuffling cards and poker chips still make my blood sing.

"Do you have an appointment?" he questions with narrowed eyes, clearly not appreciating me showing up and calling him an asshole, but he's being an asshole so I don't see how that's my fucking problem. I shake my head no. "Sounds like you-"

Before he can finish giving me the shit he wants to give me, his phone vibrates and I can hear a faintly muffled voice through the airpod he's got in. With a look of annoyance and disgust, he mutters a "mm hmm" and I already know he's probably being told to let me in. Walt told me I could come back anytime and although none of us expected it to be so soon, here I am and I'm cashing in on that open invitation. When the guy who made Joe Pesci his entire personality ends his call, he opens the door and steps aside.

"Thanks for the hospitality," I sneer. I know it's fucking stupid, but I can't help the part of me that just wants to give back every bit that was given to me. If I could get away with it, I'd love to beat the shit out of him and steal his car like he did me, but it's not why I'm here.

"Fuck up again, kid. Let me finish what I started," he says in a low tone as he elbows the sore spot on my side. His sharp jab into my ribs feels like being kicked with a cleat from the inside out, but I clench my jaw and refuse to show it. I'm not giving that dickhead the clue that it still feels like shit. I don't even get the chance to respond before he walks ahead of me to lead me to wherever the voice on the phone told him to take me.

I follow him through the short hallway, passing what must be the office on the left. The door is shut, giving this hallway the feel of a darkened tunnel to the underworld and in a way, that's exactly what it is. I'm not the only one whose life has been drastically altered by walking this same path, thinking the thrill of the game could bring enough money to make all problems just go away. Root of all evil and all that shit.

When we reach the room at the end of the hall, the scene comes into focus as wannabe Tony Montana leaves me to return to his gargoyle perch near the door. There's a couch and a tv on one side of the room, a small bar on the other, and the poker table right in the belly of the beast. At the sight of me entering the room, TJ stands from his spot on the couch, having to pull his caveman attention away from the tv. I turn my attention to the table and the lingering heavy cloud of smoke around them as TJ returns to his spot.

"Back again *so soon*, yeah?" Walt says with a smug smile around the cigar in his mouth as he throws his cards face up on the table. The four other men at the table fold, tossing their cards with a grimace while the pot goes to the house. "Junior is already in too deep over here, so he's out, aren't you, kid?"

"I'm not here for a game," I say quickly and Junior looks relieved to stay in his seat. I know the feeling of realizing you're fucked, but the longer you stay at the table the more it prolongs the inevitable. The longer you play, the longer you can pretend the whole fucking world isn't about to eat you alive.

"Then why are you in my card room? Can't be because you missed us. I never pegged you for a cake boy, but these days you never know," Walt says while the next hand is dealt, the others at the table faking uncomfortable laughter so they can appease the man who holds their collective fates in his hands. They redirect their attention to the in-coming community cards and it's hard to fight the urge to tell Junior to raise on the turn.

"There was a gold watch. In Sonnet's house, there was a gold watch in the desk of the office upstairs, and I need it back," I explain, trying not to show my hand. If they know how much it means to me, how much *she* means to me, the price will go up. Supply and demand, Walt always says as an excuse for his shitty loans and interest rates. Walt smiles as he looks over to TJ. Junior folds and blows his chance to win back some of his debt.

"TJ, I think Clif over here wants his girlfriend's watch back," Walt calls over, tossing in the ante for the next hand.

"You mean *my* new Rolly?" TJ says from the couch while he twists his wrist around, the gold watch catching the light from the tv. The idea that her father's memento was on that fucking cretan's arm added to the insult. Of course it was him. "Looks nice, but it doesn't even work. It's a pretty expensive piece of shit...kinda like you, Clif."

The room erupts in the type of laughter you expect to hear in frat houses or locker rooms. It's a room full of assholes making fun of someone, and I know I used to be one of them, but Jesus Christ, they are even more insufferable when you're *not* one of them. As TJ returns to his tv, his arms on the back of the couch, Walt keeps playing. It's like I'm not even standing there because they don't take me seriously at all.

"Look, I need that watch ok? I'll play you for it," I say the words before I get a chance to think them through. Walt puts his hand up and the dealer at the table pauses, looking at me like she knows I definitely shouldn't have said that. TJ stands up and cracks his neck side to side.

"TJ doesn't play cards. That's not why he works for me," Walt chuckles through his cigar. I look back and forth between them as they communicate with a nod I wish I could understand. I know whatever they're about to say is going to fucking blow.

"Nope, I'm not a numbers guy," TJ shrugs as he exaggerates his admiration for the watch, showing me I won't have a chance at getting it back by their means.

"Makes sense. You don't look like someone who can count without using his fingers," I quip, returning a shrug, but catching the sinister glare he shoots me. I may be willing to do anything to get that watch back, but fuck, I know it's going to hurt me one way or another.

"Make you a deal, smartass. You can have it if you can take it off me," TJ says as he stands to his full height and walks over to me. "Just you and me. We go outside and sort it out like men."

I look over to Walt, secretly hoping he'd call this what it is - stupid. *Suicide.* But he doesn't. He just motions for the dealer to continue and throws two chips into the center. Junior side-eyes me and I know he feels just as trapped as I do. I look at TJ who smiles, and I realize at this moment that Sonnet has already given up on me. I could just walk away right now and let TJ keep the Rolex. She's already lost to me, but I have to try. Maybe if I'm being honest with myself before my impending doom, I'm not willing to accept defeat just yet.

With a nod of Walt's head, I follow TJ down the green mile hallway to step outside. I expect the entire table to clear and the whole room to watch like school kids on the playground, but when they don't even move I'm hit with why. *They don't think I'll win. They think this will be over so fast it's not even worth getting up from their game.* Shit. I don't know what I'm in for, but I know how it'll feel. For some reason, I don't think it could be nearly as bad as it was to see her fall out of whatever we had. So, fuck it. We ball.

# Chapter Twenty-Five

## Clif

However I felt when I accepted the terms of this deal, I am now wading in the instant regret and full gravity of my choices. I'm not afraid to admit I would trade places with just about anyone right now, but I owe it to her to do this. If she's willing to still support Joey's appeal and get nothing in return other than the karmic balancing of the scale, I am willing to try to give her back this one token of peace.

TJ and I walk outside with mobster rent-a-cop watching from the door. There are no time outs and no one will be refereeing this match. The rules are simple. One of us leaves with the watch and the other one...well, the other one doesn't. TJ and I stand facing each other and he kisses the watch with a smile as he keeps his eyes on mine.

"When you're lying here bleeding out, I'll make sure to comfort your Little Strawberry," he taunts with a smile, his tongue darting out to lick his lower lip. "I'm gonna fuck the memory of you right out of her over and over and over."

I know it shouldn't get to me, but the flashback of his hands on her sends me to a place of blinding rage where I want to puke and slit his throat at the same time. It's all part of the game to throw me off and I fucking know it, but it takes every cell in my body not to let him into my head. I twist my neck and raise my hands like my dad taught me. *Hands up elbows down.* I keep my feet shoulder length apart and my left foot forward. Bouncing a little to shake my nerves and remain limber, I decide I'm just going to try to be defensive and tire him out so I can wait for the one perfect shot. I haven't boxed for so many years, but if I can remember enough not to let TJ beat me to a brain death, that would be a fucking miracle.

He does the same and we circle each other until he can't wait another second. TJ's fist flies out and I quickly twist at the waist and dip my knees, letting his fist hit the air. He alternates to the other hand to repeat the same motion, and I swerve it again. Chuckling, I know he can tell I'm trying my best to stay focused.

"I'm going to enjoy breaking her in too. Maybe I'll put her to work over at the motel and let the regulars take turns splittin' open that tight ass," he spits and swings, making contact with my side. I grunt, but try to ignore the imagery that makes me want to burn the entire world to the ground.

"She's off limits," I rush out, taking a chance with my right hook. He blocks it and fakes an uppercut. The moment I go to block it, he kicks my knee and I can't fight it. I go down hard onto the pavement and try to pick myself up as quickly as I can.

"No one is off limits to me, fucker," TJ threatens. "I already got my guys inside on your little baby brother. They said he's real pretty."

He rams his knee into my chest as I try to stand. I'm back on the ground, covering my neck and head while he gets in a few more rough kicks. Even if I get back up, I know he'll still have the advantage of his energy. I can taste blood in my mouth, and my already bruised torso is now wailing in agony. Every time I look up at him, I catch the glint of that fucking watch in the streetlights and it gives me a tiny jolt to hold on.

I roll quickly to miss the flat of his boot coming down on me, and with as much speed as I can muster, I get back on my feet. I'm a lot less for wear and my equilibrium is off, but I'm not taking this lying down. When he advances on me, I don't wait. All I can hear in my head is that no matter what happens with Walt, he's not going to back off my girl. *Mine.* I don't even deserve her, but fuck if I'll let this piece of shit near her ever again. I charge at TJ with every morsel of force I have left, and I take us both to the fucking ground.

Wild with primal possessiveness over a woman that might not even want me, I ram my fists into his face. I get in a few solid hits before the wind returns to his lungs and he goes for my throat. When he gets a good grip, I stop wailing on him and try to pry his maws from my neck, but he's got me. The lack of oxygen starts to make the corners of my vision fuzzy and the panic sets in. My heart rate flutters and pounds, and through it all that fucker smiles with bloody teeth. All I can think is please don't let this be the closest I ever get to that goddamn watch.

TJ sees it too, my eyes flicking to the flash of gold around his wrist, and I try to kick my legs to connect to something. There's nothing. Before I accept that this is going to end with him laughing at my unconscious body as he makes plans to visit Sonnet at her home uninvited, an idea blinds me in the limited brainwaves I have at the moment. As I continue to struggle, I remove one hand from desperately trying to free my throat and pat my front right pocket, praying to whatever gods exist that I'm right.

The second my clumsy fingertips touch the outside of my jeans, I twist my neck to get a quick gasp in to give me the last bit of energy I need. TJ is still squeezing, trying to keep me still so he can finish the job, but with how hard I'm fighting the dark, he can tell I'm not ready to go yet. I will not go quietly into the dark night and all that. Reaching into my pocket, I grasp the pearl handle of the switchblade I'm thankful they didn't take from me before this started. I'm lucky I remembered to put it in my jeans. I'm lucky as hell they didn't pat me down first.

In an instant, I jolt and everything after feels like it slows to a halt. When I move my hand, I repeat the motion again, bringing my knife into TJ's side a second time. He grunts and removes his hands from me, stumbling to a stand as he confirms it. The two stabs I got in have blended into one growing stain of red on his white t-shirt and down his pants. I stand and cough as air reenters my lungs, not letting go of the blade. With a hand over the slits in his gut, he erupts into a growl and advances on me.

"Just...give me...the fucking...watch," I grumble as I avoid letting him take me back down to the ground in a grapple. He's lunging for me, but his moves are slower and less precise.

"Fuck you," he spits, taking a swing that I didn't expect.

When his fist connects with me, I can taste the blood on my tongue, and I swing back blindly as my sweat blurs my view. He gets in one more good jab, and when I return the favor, he drops to his knees in front of me. As I shake the sweat from the hair in my face, the weight of it all hits me. I had punched TJ in the face...with the hand that held the knife. My blade had gone through his cheek to the hilt, resting under his right eye before I pulled it out. His gasps for breath turn into gargled gags as he loses consciousness and his eye begins to fill with blood. After a minute or two, there's nothing in the air but the sounds of the city again.

Shaking at the gravity of what taking a life will mean for me, I fall to my knees next to him. With his red lifeless eye staring at me, I pull the bloody watch from his heavy wrist and stumble to my feet. The sound of a slow applause ricochets off of the side of the building. I look up through at least one swollen eye to see Walt, the cigar still attached to his mouth. I brace myself for the consequences of killing his brute.

"Got your bird's trinket back then?" he says in a tone that I can't decode.

"H-He would have killed me," I reply, still catching my breath and trying to come down from the adrenaline high that's rippling through my body. At least it was preventing me from feeling the full extent of whatever TJ might have broken or bruised.

"Indeed, and probably worse to her," Walt adds with a puff. I blink hard in an effort to rid my mind with the flashing images of what TJ promised. When I open my eyes, I look down at his lifeless body. Surrounded by blood that reflects the streetlights, I keep telling myself I had no choice. "Your debt with each other is done, and so is your shit with me."

"I d-didn't have...there was no choice," I repeat out loud to accompany the chant in my head to reconcile the stain I'd have to carry on my soul now, in addition to the leverage I've just given to Walt on a silver platter.

"That was his deal. We're straight on one condition, son. The next time you need something from me, you're not paying back a debt in money. The score you gave me from that house is solid, but you and I are done dealing in dollars. You need something from me as small as a shot of whiskey, you owe me time. He might have bargained with you fair and lost, but you cost me a good employee and you'll replace him if I want you to. Do we understand each other?" he asks, waiting for me to understand that for the rest of my life, I'm one misstep away from being the new TJ. Stuck in a life of drugs, money, and anything else in the underbelly of this city Walt demands of me. I'd rather be homeless...or dead.

"Clear," I answer as I slip the watch into my pocket on the opposite side of my knife. I back up and turn to get to my car as quickly as possible. I'm almost there when I hear Walt say something in a softer tone than before.

"I'm sure I'll be seeing you again."

Driving as fast as I can, my body starts to register everything I've been through. Every part of me wars for my attention from the bruising, the pain, and the exhaustion. I'm parked crooked in front of her garage door in less than 20 minutes and I can barely see out of my right eye. My knuckles are split, my head hurts, my breathing is shaky, and all I want to do is use my last bit of energy to see her relief when I put the watch back in her hands.

Dragging myself out of the car, I stumble to her front porch and knock. Unable to support myself anymore, I lean my forehead on the door and knock again, hoping to hear the sound of her coming to answer. I open my hands and rap at the door with my palms, leaving imprints of dried blood on it. I just need to stay awake long enough to give her back what she loves. As a tear escapes my eyes, I lift my hand to knock one more time, but the door flies open, taking me with it as I tumble into her arms, pulling her to the floor.

# Chapter Twenty-Six

## Sonnet

I didn't mean to sleep for so long, but when I suddenly wake up, I see that I'm still in my room under the covers and surrounded by the mess they left. My room is still trashed, Clif is still gone, my dad's watch is stolen, and my childhood creation is still in three pieces. I wish I could have slept longer to stay in whatever dream dimension I was in to hide from this reality just a little bit longer, but for some reason, I woke up. Then I hear it. The faint sound from upstairs. *Is there someone at the door?*

I strain my ears as I get out of bed, still in the sleep shorts and sweatshirt I slipped on. Slowly stepping on each stair with only the ball of my bare feet, I squint to focus on the noise. I read once that people with Exploding Head Syndrome hear a loud noise or deafening bang in your sleep that wakes you up as if it happened in real life. At this point, I have yet to figure out if I was pulled from a dream by the dream itself or by something else. And then I hear it for real.

There's no mistaking it this time. There's someone rapping on my door in the dark and I wonder why they didn't just ring the doorbell.

It's weird. I try to look out the window, but I can't make out what I see. The sound echoes again on the door and I hear a muffled grunt. Finally making it to the other window by the door, I slide my back against the wall to see behind the curtains. There in my driveway parked at an angle is Clif's car. Clif.

I throw all caution to the side as I throw open the door. I don't have a moment to process what I'm seeing when his body falls into mine and we both hit the floor. He wraps his arms around me, digging his face into my neck and inhaling my hair. Before I get the chance to speak, I look up to see the blood on the door and I panic.

"Clif! Clif are you ok? What happened?" I say, pulling my head back to hold his face in my hands to inspect him for damage and injury. The nurse in me can't help it, and apparently neither can my heart.

"I...I didn't know where else to go...cleaned up...for you," he mumbles through the slurred words and fidgets to reach into his pocket, wincing when his bleeding knuckles rub the denim. When he pulls out his hand, my heart freezes and my eyes fill with tears. He holds the gold watch, splattered in blood, to my chest before resting his weary body back into my arms.

"What did you do? Oh my god, Clif. Come on, let's get you inside," I say through the sobs fighting their way up my throat. I slip the golden memory I thought I'd never see again over my wrist, the dragon emblem etching touching my skin for the first time in decades, and I drag Clif into the living room. While he flops onto the couch, I use my sleeve to rub the bloody handprints from my front door so I can avoid Kathy's nosy stare, and hide the evidence if what he's done has gotten the police involved somehow.

When I rush over to him, he's laying on the couch and I begin my assessment as if we were in the emergency room on my shift. He keeps his eyes closed, but alternates between wincing and grinning as I touch him. Even as an injured patient, he's such a damn flirt and I try not to smile back when I realize that even in the state he's in, he's still beautiful. He looks like a warrior. And he is.

Whatever he did, he did for me because this tiny trinket held my heart. I'd already told him to leave and he could have stayed away and waited for the will, but he didn't. *Why didn't he?* I return with a warm washcloth and a first aid kit as I clean the blood and butterfly band aid what I can. Once the blood is clear, it makes me a lot more optimistic about his current state. He's bruised, that part is pretty bad because it's on top of previous injuries, but he's going to be ok...just very sore.

"Nurse Franklin, am I going to make it?" he says softly just above a whisper when he can feel me staring at him. My hands rest on his chest, and I can feel it rise and fall with his breathing, becoming slightly heavier when he opens his unswollen eye to look at me. My lips part, unable to find the words to say first.

"Clif, what you did," I start, but he doesn't let me finish. Putting a hand over mine, I can feel the warmth of his body enveloping me from the wrist down and all I can think about is what it felt like to be completely wrapped in him.

"Hey, shhh. I had to fix us...it," he says, his other hand cupping my face as he looks directly into my eyes. His ocean waves crashing against my solid earth, flooding us both.

When I see the tears well in his eyes, mine pour and in an instant, our lips are crashing together and he's pulling me to sit on top of him. When my weight settles on him, he winces and I try to back up quickly, but his hands grip to the outside of my thighs as he grinds up into me. I gasp at how hard he is, and I can feel the side of his lips curl through our desperate kisses. I try not to hurt him, or put any weight on the parts of him I know are going to feel worse before they feel better, but every move I make to protect him, he doubles down and pulls.

"I don't want to hurt you," I whisper in between our lips.

"Then take off your clothes for me, baby," he says with a sly smile. "Let me see what I almost lost. Show me what I killed to taste again."

"Clif-" I start, but he doesn't let me finish. I don't know what he went through to get that watch and get back to me, but if what he's saying is true...*he killed for me.* I guess that makes us both killers now.

"-worth it. Come here," he rolls his hips again, and whatever part of my brain was over-analyzing what he did to sustain his injuries completely powers down to surrender to my basic instincts.

I don't have any words to fight him and I don't even want to. I lean forward to kiss him again, not even caring about the slight tinge of copper on his tongue. When I rotate a little, something pokes me in the side of the knee, something in his pocket. Reaching in for him, I pull out the pearl handled knife and know the second I see the stains on it, it's what he used to take a life tonight. When my eyes register that I'm holding the murder weapon, his hand slides up my arm to cover mine around the blade.

"I-is this..." I start to ask, but I answer myself when he nods his head. The gravity of it all threatens to crash into me, but when he slides it from my fingers, I let him. He flicks it up and down to signal that I'm still wearing a sweatshirt that he asked me to remove. I pull it over my head, only wearing a sheer bralette underneath. He sighs at the sight of me, and it makes me feel like a siren.

"Yes. I used this knife on someone tonight," Clif says as he looks at it in the light, noticing the dried blood on the silver of the blade's sharpened point. He touches the tip to my stomach, right above my belly button and when I move my hands to cover myself, he shakes his head no and applies the slightest pressure. I'm not scared. I should be scared, but my nerves come alive at the feel of it.

I let out a shameless shudder. I'm still straddling him on the couch as he lays flat, and his knife is slowly ascending up my sternum until he reaches my bralette. *Slice.* With one flick of his wrist, and a slight scratch of the blade on my skin, my small breasts are uncovered as the garment dangles on my body, cut completely open. I slip the straps down my shoulders and shrug it off, letting him see me like he wants to. His eyes touch my nipples and it feels like his hands are everywhere at the same time. I inhale.

The blade flicks my right nipple before making its descent back down my abdomen to the waist of my sleep shorts. I don't have anything underneath those, and I know it's going to become very evident when he realizes the wet spot I'm sitting in on his groin. My breasts rise and fall more rapidly as the sharp point keeps moving down. Before I can say anything, his other hand grips the crotch of my shorts right over my clit to hold them away from my body. *Slice.* In a fast rip, he cuts through the small rectangle of fabric that made my sleep shorts, well, shorts.

"There you are. There's that pretty pussy," he says as he looks directly into my core. I don't know why I suddenly have no insecurities, but sitting on top of him fully exposed in practically nothing but a skirt while his eyes drink me in makes me feel powerful. I widen my hips a little and lean back. If he's hungry for a look, I want him to get his fill and lick the plate.

"Is that what you want, Killer?" I taunt, throwing the nickname right back at him as he nods.

"Pull me out, baby. Take me out right now," he commands, and I'm relieved because I don't know how much longer I can wait. Whatever is happening, I feel like I need it more than anything. I lean back and touch the zipper of his jeans, soaked from where I was sitting, and I pull it down the track of teeth slowly enough to hear each one open for me. He's so hard that I know it must hurt being caged in those pants, and when I free his perfect cock, all I want to do is impale myself with it.

"Good girl, now bring that pussy up here and sit on my face," Clif growls, getting harder as he stares at me and how close he is to being inside me again. I stand and walk to him while he keeps a hand on my leg, like some part of him has to keep touching me. I flinch when he stabs the knife into the coffee table to free up both of his hands. When I walk over to him and move to lift my leg, he shakes his head, and I pull back embarrassed that he changed his mind. "No, baby, face the other way. You're going to take me down your throat, aren't you?"

I nod obediently, thankful for the chance to make him proud and show my gratitude for what he did for me. My knight in battle. I turn my body and as he instructed, I sit my full weight on his face, feeling his mouth close around me instantly. We both groan at the same time, and I lean forward, slipping him past my lips and as deeply down my throat as I can get him.

We stay still in that position for just a moment before he starts to move his hips and I roll mine in response. It's like a race to see who can stay focused enough on their task at hand while being stimulated beyond comprehension. As I bounce my head over him, I move my hand down to cup him. He returns the sensation overload by grabbing my ass with both hands to hold me to him and open me up wider. I freeze when he runs his tongue from my clit to my pussy...and then to my ass. I gasp, and he uses my mouth's sudden opening to thrust his cock deeper at the same time he pushes a finger into my core.

Before my orgasm can rip through me, he slows his pace and pumps his finger in and out. When I groan to complain, he rolls his hips, pushing into my mouth deeper and past the back of my tongue. I fight the urge to gag as the drool gives into gravity and seeps from the corners of my lips and down his base to cover the grip I have him in. As my climax begins to build again, he pulls his finger out and teases my tight ring of muscle while he returns his tongue to my pussy.

When he pushes into my backside, I groan around his length and he hisses an inhale. It feels so good to bring him to the brink with me, and I am pleasantly surprised at how much I definitely don't hate the attention he's giving to a part of me I've never thought to explore. As I bring my head up and down, my moans fight to escape my mouth as he works his magic tongue and fingers everywhere. The closer I get to exploding, the more I shamelessly ride his face and push my ass back into his finger, which has turned into two. When our speed increases, I can feel him start to pulse.

"Drink me down, Killer. Every drop, ok?" Clif mutters from under me, his fingers still slamming into me. I nod around him. "Say it, baby."

"I'll drink every drop," I say in a breath when I pull his cock out of my mouth just long enough to answer and gasp. He pushes my head back down onto him and sucks my clit into his mouth.

I scream out when my orgasm crashes through me with a force I've never felt, and as the vibrations from my voice ripple around his length, he fists a handful of my hair to hold me still. Within seconds he's spilling down my throat. As gravity pulls his cum down his shaft, threatening to leave my lips, I softly hollow my cheeks to bring it back into my mouth, and all the way down like I promised.

When the waves of pleasure slow to a crawl, Clif helps me to stand. I forget I'm completely bare save for the cut sleep shorts that I wear around my waist like a skirt. He braces himself on the arm of the couch and stands, still completely dressed as he tucks himself back into his pants. He pulls the knife from the table and returns it to his front pocket. I notice at the same time he does that there's still blood on his clothes, and I take a moment to process the recent development to our situation.

"Clif, what you did for me...I...thank you," I say, disappointed that there's nothing I can say that will fully express the vital importance of what he's risked. He must pick up on it because he tucks my hair behind my ear. "You didn't have to do that."

"Yes, I did. I never wanted to hurt you, Sonnet. I'd do anything to take it back," he replies with a voice so sincere, it makes me want to believe anything and everything. He could use it to tell me the sky was purple, and I'd nod at him with a smitten grin and hearts in my eyes. With a shake of my head, I try to snap myself out of the cloud 9 haze that we seemed to be wrapped in, but I can't.

"No one's ever fought for me before. Or...umm..." I trail off, not knowing how to finish the sentence. When he knows what I'm thinking, he takes a deep breath to brace himself before he scoops me into his arms and walks up the stairs to the bathroom. "Clif!"

Reaching the doorway, he sets me down and starts the shower as I help him out of his clothes. When we're both bare and surrounded by the steam, we step into the water, wrapped in each other's arms. As he leans back to frame my face with his hands, I can't help but inhale sharply when I see the bruises littered throughout his tattooed torso. Pulling my attention back to his face, he kisses my forehead and stares into my eyes, like he's trying to tell me something without using any words. When his lips part, my gaze drifts to their perfect fullness and what they just did to my body.

"Do you remember that asshole that grabbed you at the motel?" he asks, with a look like it pains him to even remember it. I furrow my brows at the sheer thought of that night and what he threatened to do to me. I nod my head slowly, nervous at what Clif has to tell me. "He told me tonight what he wanted to do to you. He told me and I went blank. Walt said I had to take the watch from the guy myself, so I did...I killed him. I'd do it again if I could. He's not going to touch you ever again."

"Oh god, are you ok? Clif are you-I'm so-"

"-no, don't say it," he says as the water from his hair travels down, dripping from his chin to my chest. "This was my shit and I pulled you into it."

I smile as I pull his gaze from my bare chest back to my eyes, and his hard length presses against my stomach in reflex. He shares a grin, and I can't help but remind him of the obvious fact as I slide my hands down his body to wrap my fingers around his cock. When I do, his eyes roll back and he lets me push him against the tile.

"You weren't a killer until you met me, remember, Jack?" I say in a breathy tone.

"Are you saying you corrupted me?" he asks playfully as his hands find my hips. "And I was completely innocent until I met you?"

"I made you a killer," I whisper, partly in apology, but I can't help that I'm glad he removed the threat to my life from someone who would have taken everything from me before I died. He shakes his head and I tilt mine in question.

"You made me a knight, Dragon Queen," he says with a fist over his heart as he slowly lowers himself to his knee under the stream. I want to laugh at how silly it is, but the idea that he chose to do what he did, how is he really any different from a warrior in my books? When he looks up at me through his one good eye, I see the pain he went through voluntarily for me, and my heart flutters in my chest.

"And what reward do you seek?" I ask like a queen, running my nails through his wet black hair. I can't help but be amazed that not only is this man dark, tall, and tattooed, but he knows about the book series that made me fall in love with fantasy worlds and romance. I try to tell my mind to slow down, that I've only known him a short while and it's been full of crime and violence, but when I stop thinking, my heart answers the call.

"To belong. Not only to your royal guard, but to you," Clif answers without taking his eyes away from me. His hands travel from my feet up my legs and to my hips, until he rests his forehead against my abdomen, over my womb. "Keep me, Sonnet, please."

Taken aback by the plea I've never even dreamed I'd hear, I fist the back of his hair to bring his head back. The movement isn't aggressive or rushed, but it feels important, like we're signing a blood contract and we don't know what the fine print says. I don't know every secret he has, but I can't fight the sheer magnetism I feel towards him. It's the big bang of the universe, but between two souls. When his chin is up and I stare down at him on my shower floor, he has a vulnerability on his face. He knows this could slice his spirit, but he's displaying his neck to me anyway in complete surrender and unwavering loyalty, and it's the most beautiful thing I've ever seen.

"Knights kneel. Kings and queens bow to no one," I whisper, lowering myself to my knees to meet him on the tile floor beneath the warm rainwater shower. His brows flick upward in surprise and arousal when I kiss him gently, then turn my body to press my ass into his groin. He groans in pleasure and gratitude as his hands snake their way around my front, one finding my breast and the other, cupping my pussy in ownership.

"Mine," he growls, his lips tickling the shell of my ear as his hands begin to work.

"Mine," I growl back possessively, pushing back into him until I feel his cock slide through the wetness of my lips. I tighten my thighs and rock back and forth to coat him as he moves to rub circles on my clit, using his thumb and forefinger to pinch my nipple.

When I lean forward to put my hands on the floor, his length aligns perfectly. I don't know who moves first, but in seconds Clif is buried inside of me to the hilt, and he's leaning over me pumping deeper than he's ever been. As we both cry out in pleasure, the sound echoing through the empty house, I can't help but stare at his inked hands on the floor next to mine as he covers me. With each push of his hips flush against my ass, I watch the water clean the dried blood from his knuckles and under his fingernails.

I raise one hand above my head to pull the hair at the back of his head, and he bites down on the soft spot where my neck and shoulder meet. I feel like a wild animal, and after we've both crossed the line and become murderers, maybe that's all we are anymore. Killing for survival. Killing for territory. Killing for love. One of his hands leaves the floor next to mine to return to my clit and I can't hold in much longer. With every thrust, I push back, and it feeds my frenzy where all I can think about is wanting him in every way all at the same time.

I feel his abs tighten on my back, the brink of my climax braced together like we're the base and treble bars of sheet music. I turn my head to his behind me and with a bruising kiss that feels like the point of no return, we both erupt. Falling into the weightless dimension of blissful exhaustion that follows mind blowing moments of pleasure, we share a kiss and help each other to stand. In a mutual appreciation for each other and our aftercare, we wash quickly as the water begins to lose its heat. Wrapping each other in warm towels, Clif kisses my head and we look at each other in a new light; one that says everything even when we're saying nothing.

# Chapter Twenty-Seven

## Clif

It's been four days. I've been back and forth to my place a few times to grab clothes and throw away my junk mail. Sonnet has gone back to work, mostly the night shift, and it's sexy to see her back to wearing the scrubs I saw her in for the first time. I've helped her clean out the house entirely, and the realtor has already brought another couple out to take a look while hinting to us that it'll most likely be a quick sale.

A couple days ago. I got a call from Joey just to check in, but he was thrilled as hell when I told him that I got the money for his appeals case on the way. I didn't tell him how exactly, but I said it would be soon and it's enough hope for him to hold onto for now. Sonnet spoke to the lawyer again yesterday and she's feeling good about the timeline. It feels oddly calming to be in a relationship that's so normal and domestic, but it's like we've been this way forever. For me, it usually feels that way right before something fucks it all up, but I try not to let my paranoia get to me and sabotage what we have. When my phone rings as I'm heading back from my place to hers, the feeling settles in my gut as I accept an unexpected call from the jail.

"Hey, baby brother, what's-"

"-Clif, you gotta get me outta here, man," Joey says with a rushed whisper like he's trying to hide his voice. I've heard my brother stressed out and anxious, but never like this, even on the day he was booked.

"What happened?" I ask with a stern focus. I pull my BMW into the parking lot of the nearest convenience store and turn the radio off. With the silence inside the car opposing the hustling white noise of the outside world, I still my entire body and will myself not to panic.

"I'm ok, but they fucking stabbed me right in the gut, man. It was shallow, but fuck. He said something about it being for PJ or TJ, and if the CO hadn't turned the corner, they would have fucking killed me. How much more time do I have in here. I need out, Clif, please," Joey begs quietly, his voice shaking and it slices me open on the inside.

"Fucking TJ...ok look, I'll take care of it, ok? Please trust me. I'll come see you as soon as I can and I'll bring answers or the fucking attorney. I'm going to fix this, Joey. I'm going to make it right no matter what," I promise him without telling him exactly what that means because honestly I don't fucking know yet either. All I know is I can't let him die in there. I can't let him keep paying the price for my shit, and I hate myself for reveling in even a single moment of peace while he's locked up in my place.

"I know you're working on it, man. I know, but hurry ok?" he says softly and then the line cuts out either for time, or because he doesn't want the guys to hear him break under their pressure.

When I pull into Sonnet's driveway, she opens the door for me and just like the picture perfect delusion we've been bubbled in, she waits for me to pick her up into my arms and carry her inside. It's been our routine. Working, having meals at the table, making love and fucking all over the house afterward, and then falling asleep sometimes when I'm still inside of her. Ever since I fucking met her, even with the illegality of everything we've gotten into, it's been the best part of my life. But when I see her at the door, her smile falls as I walk right in, passing her to sit right on the couch in the living room. She follows me and sits with a hand on my back.

"Hey, what's wrong?" she asks with a comforting voice that I know people in pain on her shift are lucky to hear. That would be enough to make anyone start to feel optimistic about their condition. Her hand does circles over my black shirt, which is now a little damp from the anxiety sweats I drove home through.

"Joey called. Someone inside jumped him for what I did to TJ," I answer, my head in my hands. I can't even look at her because I'm petrified she'll see how fucking much I hate myself for all of this. "They could have killed him because of me."

"Hey, no. It's not your fault, Clif, you can't-"

"Of course it's my fucking fault! He's sitting in that cell because I roped him into my scumbag shit and he was too good to let me pay the price. I got you sucked into it too. Everyone I love-" I pull in a sharp inhale the second I slip and I know she heard it too. Putting my head in my hands, I just breathe and fight the sharp hardness in my throat. I hate the urge to crumble and hide right now, but she's holding onto me. Even though I don't deserve it, or her, I feel grateful to not be alone in it all.

"Clif?" she says so softly that I can't help but look up at her. "I won't let your brother go through this, ok? I already got a call and I was trying to tell you I'm heading over to talk to them about her estate in an hour...and I love you too."

"Baby, you know there are other people in the world that can offer you so much more. You deserve *more*," I admit to her and to myself, swallowing the lump in my throat back down and steeling my body for the impact of her realizing it too.

"All the money in the world won't buy the knee you bent, my king. You killed to protect me, remember? What could I ask for more than that type of love? It's everything I've ever dreamed of and honestly, I thought the whole 'burn the world for her' thing was also just a 'written by women' thing. But you're real and you're here, and we swore we would belong to each other. I already promised I'd help, ok? And that was before I knew I loved you. Let me save you this time," Sonnet says while one rogue tear rolls down my cheek as I stare into the warm serenity that only exists in her eyes. She is everything I don't deserve. Everything I'm not worthy of having, but for some reason I don't understand, she's here and I'm fucking overwhelmed with what it feels like to be in her care.

"I love you, Sonnet. I love you so fucking much, and there isn't anything I wouldn't do for you," I vow, touching my forehead to hers. "Thank you."

When she pulls me into an embrace, wrapping her arms around me tightly, I can't help but feel the fire ignite in my chest. With the look I've seen in her eyes, I know now more than ever that she's a fighter just as much as I am. Although I can feel her breasts pushed against me, the way we're holding each other feels like more than sex. I don't know if I've ever known what love feels like until right now, but it feels like I got hit with a blinding light; like I've seen an angel on earth and can't shake the awe.

Pulling back, she kisses me sweetly and stands to straighten her signature blue scrubs. Her copper hair is pulled back, highlighting her beautiful smile, the one I will prove every day that I am worthy of. I will be the man she deserves. She grabs her keys off the table and points to the kitchen.

"There's an Italian sub on the counter for lunch, ok? I'm going to head over to the office on my way to work to talk to them about the will and estate and as soon as I know anything, I'll text you," she says, kissing me again as she passes. "I love you."

"I love you too," I say, the phrase still feeling foreign on my tongue, but so right when I say it to her. I've never told a woman I loved them except my mom before she bailed and I barely even remember that. I don't think anyone could make me feel love except Sonnet.

She smiles and sips from her ridiculously big stickered cup before leaving. The moment she's gone, it's like she took all of the warmth with her. Bill Withers was right when he sang that "ain't no sunshine when she's gone". Her house is quiet and without her, it's just a cold building. There's nothing without her anywhere and then I realize it's exactly how I feel too. Shit. She really is it for me. When this is all finished one day soon, I can't wait for Joey to meet her. I have a feeling the minute they start going on about fantasy books, he'll love her too. *Like a sister*. It better fucking be like a sister.

# CHAPTER TWENTY-EIGHT

## Sonnet

After a solid blood-curdling scream of frustration, I have been sitting in my car for almost an hour while I process what the fuck just happened in that office, and what I learned about the version of Gloria Franklin that she kept hidden from all of us. The pieces and words keep rolling through my head, but no matter how hard I try, part of me fights to accept the inevitable. I guess I have to because according to them, there's no other choice. *Debt. Repayment. Probate court. Debt. Settle. Estate. Debt.*

I'd always thought my mother was too proud of a woman to allow herself to live in a nursing home or assisted living facility, but if what I just learned is true, then that was a lie. My mother may have been proud, but she was also apparently drowning in debt so deep that she almost lost the house. Instead, she moved me in to help her, and without even realizing it, I paid the bills that kept her afloat. I won't lie and say that I wasn't hoping her estate would help to repay what I'd spent on her, but this is the Tworst case scenario.

Between what's left of her estate including the house, I'm left with under three thousand dollars after everything. I promised Clif I'd help him with Joey and I still intend on doing that, but it'll take a little longer. They told me that if I can get just 15% or so above what I expect for the house, then I'll be able to cover the downpayment on a new place and help Clif. I know it's a lot to ask for him to wait, but if he can't, then I'll take out a loan to make sure he's ok and keep my word. If we're going to make this work long term, then we have to be able to handle tough shit like this. I just wish there was another way, and by that I mean, if Walt hadn't cleaned out Mom's jewelry, I would have been way less fucked than I am now.

Dreading the phone call I have to make on my way to work, I pull out of the parking lot and call Clif, who I saved in my phone as "Mine" with three emojis next to it - a knife, a black heart, and a crown. I almost don't want him to pick up so I can resort to hiding behind a text, especially after his brother's call today, but we promised no more secrets. When he picks up, I can tell he must have accidentally fallen asleep on the couch.

"Hey, baby," he says with a groggy voice that makes me warm. "How'd it go?"

"It's not what I expected," I start with a heaviness in my chest that makes it hard to breathe without wanting to cry. I can hear him still, waiting for me to elaborate.

I tell him everything from Mom's assets to her debt settlement and then finally to what it means for us, and for his brother's appeal. I feel like I can hear his defeat and heartbreak in the silence on his side of the line, and my mind settles on what to do.

"I'm going to take out a loan tomorrow, ok? I'll pay it back when the house sells, but a quick fifteen thousand would get Joey some help. If I just-"

"-no."

"Ok, how about twenty? Then we get him a really good lawyer, and-" I suggest, but the way he said it sounded so final. Like he decided something without me, and I'm not going to like it.

"I'm not taking your money, Sonnet. I'm not going to let you go take out a loan for this. It's not right. We both know if Walt hadn't stripped this house of everything of value that wasn't bolted to the fucking ground, this wouldn't be happening. I'm going to handle it. I can't ask you to take part in it anymore," he says with a resolve that scares me.

"But we're together and I want to handle this together," I say with my tears, losing the battle behind my eyes.

"...Baby, I can't ask you to do that anymore. Walt told me if I needed money, he'd let me work for him. I'm going to do it, and I need you to stay out of it."

"Fat fucking chance, Clif, no. Fuck no. We promised and fine, I don't have to take out a loan, but we could get Joey moved for now and then when the house sells-" I plead with him, but he cuts me off again, making me feel frantic like I'm losing him to his pride and there's nothing I can do about it.

"-I can't. He can't wait and I promised him. He's my family, Sonnet. I have to do this for him," he says firmly and I can hear movement on the phone now. He's already getting in his car and I know he's on his way to see his brother or Walt. Without him having to say it, I know what comes next. "I'm going to stay at my place for a while to work this out with Walt. I don't want him anywhere near you or this house."

"But I love you," I cry, not even caring that he can hear it. "Can't we find another way? Please, Clif, just wait for me to come home."

"It'll just be harder on us, baby. I have to do this. I love you too, but I need some time to handle the shit I got Joey in. If something happened to him, I'd never forgive myself and if something happened to you, I'd never forgive myself. You can't keep saving me. I have to take care of this alone," he explains and I understand what he's saying, but I feel like my heart is ripping in two. "Please. Say you understand."

"How long?" I choke out, not even caring that the person in the car beside me at the red light is watching me sob at my phone. The loss I feel is so deep, and I can't help but imagine that maybe the karmic balance of everything is real and I deserve to lose this.

"I don't know," he answers honestly, like we said we would. Before I get the chance to say anything, he cuts in. "I wish we met another way. Thank you for everything, Sonnet. I love you. Be happy."

"Clif, I-" I start, but the call ends.

I twist the wheel in the middle of the road to whip a u-turn into the parking lot of a strip mall. I scream again into the quiet enclosed car and curse every single moment that will be stolen from us because of my mother. I don't know what Walt will have Clif do, but I know it won't be legal, and he'll be able to hold that over his head for blackmail the rest of his life. Who knows if Walt will even let an appeal go through before having someone hurt Joey beyond recognition on the inside. If Joey's already been stabbed by someone on TJ's behalf, maybe Walt's reach isn't as far as any of us thought.

Digging in my purse, I pull out a packet of tissues to wipe away any last bits of mascara that happened to stay on my lashes after my meltdown. Holding my phone in my shaking hands, my brain races through everything I have at my disposal to change the course of this train as it derails. Every moment of romantic love I've ever felt in my life has been with Clif, and I'm not going to let this happen without a fight. He killed for me, and now it's time I fight for him.

I call work and let them know I'm not coming to my shift tonight, and with everything I've been through with my mother, they don't put up a fight. With that taken care of, I look at my reflection in the rear view mirror. My eyes are red rimmed and puffy, but my cheeks are coming back to their fair color as I transition to brainstorming. Looking around my car, I start to think of what I can do aside from taking out a loan to secure a quick lump of cash. I can't ask for an advance on my paycheck, but maybe I could try to get one on the house.

As my breathing returns to normal, I sift through my purse again for some chapstick when my fingers brush by something I'd forgotten about. The moment I see it, an idea abruptly enters my mind and answers all of my questions from the past hour. For the first time, I have a slight tinge of hope that I actually can save the Dragon King for once.

Whipping my car out onto the road, I put a quick search into Maps and find every shop nearby that can help me. Near the destination, I screenshot the phone number of the best lawyer that popped up on the search Clif and I did last night. Holding my dad's watch in my hands, I kiss the face of it. As much as it means to me, it's a token of a love I lost and the only way I can stop it from happening again.

# CHAPTER TWENTY-NINE

# Clif

I spent the night at my place. Tomorrow I'm handing myself over to Walt to negotiate a deal for the loan I need to help Joey out of the fucking quicksand he jumped in for me. I know I didn't have to cut things with Sonnet like I did, but I need the time to clear my head and I can't do that when all I can think of is how much she consumes me, and how much I've needed that. I don't deserve to have her while Joey suffers. With the lawyer we looked into, I'm thinking I could ask Walt for a job instead of time served, and maybe with a decent smash and grab or a couple debt collections as he calls them, I can be back to bed with her.

Sitting on my couch, I realize how fucking pathetic my situation has gotten. I guess it takes peeking over the fence to even notice how greener the neighbor's grass really is, and for a little while, I saw what a life with her would feel like. Even with all the stress and danger, I've never eaten or slept so fucking good. Shit, I actually saw what I could look like if I was happy for once and not just blissfully high or drunk off my ass.

I light up a cigarette and scroll through my messages, the only sound in the shitty apartment being what's happening outside of it. The screeching of tires, the yelling of random people as their BAC levels rise far past the legal limit, the slamming of other doors down the hall. But inside my place, it's eerily quiet like the calm before a tornado. Joey used to tell me about it when he visited his new girl after she moved south of Chicago and he experienced his first green sky siren. He said there was a heaviness to the air, and a quiet like the earth was waiting for something, or bracing itself for the unpredictability of the funneled storm. Well, that's how this shit feels right now.

After two smokes and a bit of whiskey, I go back and forth with myself about calling her again. I know I just have to keep my distance for a while until I'm done with whatever shit I'm about to get into, but it fucking sucks. She thinks it would be fine, but she doesn't know these assholes like I do. They see something they can turn for profit and they take it, just like TJ threatened. If anyone knows I'm with her, she becomes part of whatever deal they strike with me and if I don't make it out, I don't want them collecting her to pay off what's left of my debt. Just the thought of it makes me want to set everything on fire.

The thought of me dying on Walt's payroll turns my stomach more than the nicotine and alcohol dinner I just downed. I have to remember to get a guarantee on Joey's appeal before I agree to anything, and I have to find a way to keep her happy, even if it can't be with me. Wishing there was a way to keep at least a part of her with me, the thought instantly molds itself into an impulsive plan, and I grab my phone to text someone who owes me a fucking favor - and that list is really short anyway.

It didn't even take an hour for Sebastian to get in and get his shit set up on the coffee table. When he took out his wrinkled sketchpad, I described the idea as best as I could remember. I'd only gotten a couple looks at the inspiration for it, so between my shitty memory and the buzz I was feeling, I did my best. It only takes my man Seb a few tries before we settle on the best version of it. I lay back on my couch with my shirt tossed onto the floor, and I let him get to work on the tattoo that makes me think of her. If I never see her again, carrying her over my heart is the best I can do to remember the only time in my life I didn't feel like a failure.

"What's her name?" Seb asks, making the same type of small talk he uses for most of the other tattoos he's given me. I debate for a second if I can trust him with her name. It doesn't seem like much, but when you're getting the shit kicked out of you for information, any bit could save you from internal bleeding. Remembering the name in the books she loves, I think of how Sonnet would look on a golden throne, and I smile. The image fucking suits her.

"Althea," I groan as the needle drags over my chest.

"Sounds hot," Seb raises his eyebrows, but when he looks over at me, I'm not sharing his expression. "I mean, not for me though. My Nadia keeps me busy."

The rest of the session is pretty quiet. I try not to let anyone in when I'm feeling cagey, and Seb is good at reading people's body language which is good for him in his line of work. Patching me up, Seb and I exchange a nod. He throws his equipment back in the case and leaves the pile of bloody inked paper towels on the coffee table. Looking back as he heads for the door, we share a light embrace, careful not to disturb my new addition.

Slipping back onto the couch in the same spot I'd just laid in for the two hour session, I close my eyes and let the sounds adjust now that the buzz of the machine is gone. I hold the bottle of whiskey to my lips and take another swig to settle the dull ache in my chest that's either from my tattoo or missing her, or both. It's only minutes before I feel the weight of exhaustion drag my eyelids down and as I surrender to it, I enjoy my last night of freedom.

The sound of my phone ringing wakes me up, and immediately the way I sat up faster than my pounding head disorients the fuck out of me. As I regain balance, I notice two things at the same time. First, it's past 1pm. Two, I'm getting a call from Greensburg Correctional Facility. The call makes me nervous and I immediately feel my nerves start to tighten and send tiny pins and needles all over my body. Accepting the call as quickly as my shaking finger can swipe, I hope for him to be ok.

"H-hey, Joey," I manage to spit out as I sit up straight and swig a shot of whiskey.

"Man, you really did it. I mean, I didn't doubt you, but fuck, you really did it," Joey says with a rushed exhale, like he used to sound when he was happy and excited about something.

"Right, uhhh...what exactly did I do again?" I ask, genuinely confused at what I'm hearing to the point I pull the phone from my ear to check the number on the screen. Then I blink to make sure I'm not still fucking passed out. When those two things seem to be firing on all cylinders, I wait, stumped.

"The lawyer you got me is so fucking good, she got me moved to solitary for safety reasons and she says I probably won't be in here much longer because her whole fucking team is working on my case, man! She's really going to get me out! It's for real! Thank you!" he almost shouts into the phone. I can hear him fighting back the urge to cry out of relief, but he's keeping it down. Me though? My tears start falling before he even finishes.

"I don't know-" I start to tell him that I can't explain it, but then it hits me like a truck. I know exactly how this happened. *My girl.* God damn it. "I mean, I told you I'd fix this, brother. Now you do whatever that lawyer lady tells you and I'll see you in court and out of there soon."

"Fuck yeah! That chick tells me to bark, I'm fucking barking," Joey laughs and it feels like it's been decades since I've heard that sound. Even though we're not out of the clear yet, a small part of me heals just from hearing it. "I love you, brother."

"I love you too, man." I say with a quiver in my voice that I'm not ashamed of.

*My fucking girl.* I told her no loans, but the fact that she behaved like the little brat she is makes me fall even deeper in love with her. She did this for me. She got the money for a lawyer to help a guy she's never met file an appeal strictly because he's my brother and she loves me. I have a brother who took the fall for me, a girl who did what was necessary to save him, and an overwhelming feeling that I don't deserve either of them. What did I ever do that made me worthy of their love? Whatever it was, it was the only good thing I've ever done.

Hopping in the shower and peeling the patch off my ink, I wear it even more proudly now. The ink that reminds me of her like a permanent coat of arms. A forever sigil for my dragon queen. I can't get my shit together fast enough as I throw on a clean, but wrinkled, black t-shirt and black jeans. Combing my fingers through my damp hair, I slip my knife and phone into my pockets before swiping the keys off the table and rushing out the door. I'm going to redden her ass for not listening, and then kiss it better for not listening.

# CHAPTER THIRTY

## Sonnet

As much as it hurt to part with Dad's watch, the feeling of how right it was overshadowed the pain when the cash in my hands turned into the only way of keeping Joey safe and preventing Clif from signing his own death warrant. I'd tried calling him before my shift to tell him that I had it handled, but he never answered. Now that I'm home, showered, and in my sweats, everything I'd been through in the last 48 hours left my body in a state of mental and physical exhaustion.

Remembering I hadn't even eaten in almost half a day, I drag my feet to the refrigerator and wade in the instant flood of relief when the pizza from a couple days ago was still in there. My mouth salivated just picturing the pepperoni, bacon, and green pepper thin crust and I didn't even think twice before reaching into the box and pulling a few slices out. With the refrigerator door propped open with my hip, and cold pizza in my right hand, I reach in to grab the last gatorade in the back. Humming to myself with my miniature burst of energy from the late night snack, I almost miss the sound of the front door.

I stand up fast, having no idea what to expect with everything that's happened, but I gasp when Clif comes around the corner looking like a dreamy personification of darkness and danger. I'm still holding pizza and gatorade when he rushes me and I drop them all to the floor as he lifts me by my hips and sits me on the kitchen table, standing between my legs. He's holding my face in his hands and with a touch of his forehead to mine, I can feel the heat off of his body as my heart begins to race and my breathing stutters.

"What did you do, Killer?" he asks with the minty warmth of his breath brushing my lips like a painting. "What did you do for the money?"

"I...I sold Dad's watch," I answer hesitantly. I know he'll be angry, but there's nothing I wouldn't do for him, and if I had to make the choice again, I'd do it all the same to keep him. When the words leave my lips, he pulls his face from mine and his eyes search me for something. Maybe it's regret. Maybe it's resentment. But if he can see what I feel through my hazel eyes, all he'll see is love. When he registers the truth, his face softens and his brows turn up in hurt.

"Baby, why? This was my mess and that watch meant everything to you...I'll get it back again. I swear I'll-" he starts, but I put a hand to his lips to stop him so I can explain what he needs to know.

"There's nothing that means more to me than being with you. I would do it again. You asked me to keep you and I gave myself in return, remember? I loved my Dad, but he's gone and it took the risk of losing you for me to realize I'd trade anything to spend forever with you. I can't lose you too. I don't need the watch back, Clif, I just want you," I ramble through the tears in my eyes as I lay bare everything I have in my heart for him.

When he pauses, my soul drops and I hope I'm not too late. I tell myself not to jump to conclusions, but every cell in my body freezes as

I imagine the strong possibility that he's coming to give me a proper goodbye for closure after already swearing his loyalty to Walt. Every second he's silent, I feel my heart rip open a little more. When I look into his eyes expectantly, readying myself for the killshot I've clearly left myself open for, the side of his mouth lifts in a soft smirk and those baby blues show a glassy shine.

"Am...am I too late?" I ask sheepishly. "Did Walt...are you-?

"-No baby, you're perfect. I never made it to Walt's," he admits and when I quirk a brow nervously with a hint of curiosity, he elaborates. "I drank a little too much liquid courage when I left here because I thought I had to lose you to keep you and Joey safe. When I woke up, Joey called and said you got him moved to solitary. He said that the lawyer we wanted was already barking commands at the staff and telling him he was going to be out soon. I've never heard him so relieved and...and you did that for him and for me."

"No Walt?" I repeated to hear him confirm it out loud to reassure me that the risk of losing him is over. "You're staying?"

"No Walt," he says again with a smile and a hand on my cheek. "I belong to you, Little Killer. My Dragon Queen. For as long as you'll have me."

"I'll always have you and you'll always have me. I love you, Clif," I speak with my whole heart as a tear escapes my eyes.

Without another word, he kisses his immeasurable devotion into my skin from my lips to the small space beneath my earlobe. Licking a line from my collarbone up the side of my neck, he returns to my lips with a groan that vibrates into my mouth. My legs tighten around his waist as we solidify our need with another deep kiss that's less of a kiss and more of an act to devour. I barely have a moment to run my fingers through the back of his hair as he pulls my top over my head.

The second my copper hair shakes loose from the sweatshirt as it falls to the floor, I reach for his belt. I can't live for another minute without his warm skin on mine. When people write scenes that say the lovers feel a frenzy or a sex craze, I have a firm understanding of it at this exact moment. My mind is blank except for the primal part of me pumping through my blood that demands we connect in the most basic way we were designed to. As if he can sense the need seeping through my pores like pheromones, he puts his palm over my heart to lay me back on the table mixing sensual and sexual in a delicious sensation that makes me feel a heartbeat in my chest and in my clit.

As my back rests on the cool tabletop, I hear his belt whip out of the loops of his jeans, and the zipper pull down before they join my sweatshirt on the floor. The way he looks at me while his fingers curl around my waistband to peel off my sweatpants is purely devious, and I can already feel my arousal slowly drip from me. I don't even flinch at the chill air that hits my bare pussy when I'm completely naked on my kitchen table. All I can do is hold my breath when he reaches behind his head to pull his black t-shirt off.

When his full body is on display, I gasp at what I see, bringing myself up on my elbows. There's what looks like fresh ink on his chest. And it's...it's...

"Clif, is that-?"

"-oh, yeah I tried to get it as close as I remembered in case...well, I didn't know what would happen with Walt and I wanted you with me, so I-"

I didn't let him finish before I pulled him to me. Over his heart was an exact replica of the dragon emblem my father had on the back of his Rolex. I gave up the watch for him and he found a way to let me keep the most important part of it. I don't know if I truly believed in fate before this second, but how can I ever deny it again. My heart soars and I hook my hand around his neck to crash my lips to his, his hardened length already pressing at my entrance.

He rocks his hips in small bursts, teasing my slit and I groan with anticipation. It makes him smile at my impatience and how he can turn me into such a whining puddle of greed. He pulls back and stands straight up, yanking my hips to his, but not entering me like I expected. I almost growl with how much every cell in my body wants him to fuck me already. With a knowing smile, he runs his hands up to my breasts and cups both, moving his fingers to pinch my nipples at the same time, and I swear in my head that I might spontaneously combust if he continues to edge me like this. There is now a wet spot under my ass from how soaked I am for him, and I start brainstorming what I can do to convince him to let me feel him inside me immediately. So naturally, I resort to begging.

"Clif, please," I plead with him and he smiles, clearly pleased with himself having accomplished exactly what he wanted.

"You want me inside you, baby?" he taunts, using a hand to grip his cock and teasingly rub the head up and down my pussy. I can't help myself as I nod with shameless desperation. Abandoning the motion of his cock, he brings both hands up and bends my legs at the knees, delivering clear instructions, exactly like I need him to. "Show me, then. Hold your thighs open as wide as you can and show me your pretty pussy. Show me what's all mine now."

I moan as he tells me what to do, and looking directly at the blue eyed king wearing my dragon emblem over his heart, I oblige. Putting my hands under my bent knees, I pull my legs open as wide as I can go and don't stop even when I feel the burn of the muscles in my inner thighs. I feel another drop of pleasure slide from my core and down my ass as his eyes drink in the sight of me shamelessly spread open on my kitchen table. Even if he's not touching me, it feels like it with the way he's looking at every inch of me, no secrets of my body between us and he groans in approval.

"That's my girl," he says, coming closer again and I welcome the warmth of his cock near my entrance. "And this is my pussy."

It's the only warning I get before he slams into me, burning my bare back on the table as I am forcefully nudged up. I almost laugh at how euphoric the pain is. You could break my arm and as long as Clif was fucking me like this, I don't know if it would even register. His thrusts don't let up as he rocks his hips into me and licks my body with his stare from my purple polished toes to my face contorted in the throes of ecstasy.

With my hands holding my thighs apart, he has no trouble pushing his palm into my abdomen and using his thumb to circle my clit. When his touch meets my bundle of nerves, the jolt through my nervous system makes me certain I can see paradise, and I cry out.

"That's right, baby. Now, say my name," he instructs. "I want you to come with me deep in your cunt and my name on your lips."

"C-Clif. Oh my god, Clif," I stutter. I don't know if all of my brain cells have ceased firing, but I've become nothing but a cavewoman at this point; a willingly mindless slave to my ID. At the sound of my words, he groans out loud and picks up the pace, both of us speeding toward the climax we need.

"Yes, baby. Say it again. I want to hear it again," he commands, pumping in and out of me while my back burns and the kitchen fills with the symphony of our bodies crashing together; the most primitive percussion.

I can't help it. I pulse once and scream his name over and over through an orgasm that seems to go on forever. He comes shortly after I do with a ravenous roar that sounds like a territorial victory. With us both gasping for breath, and the ache of my position starting to set in, he pulls out of me and my brows crease when I feel what he's doing. With a determined look on his face, he lowers his fingers to where he's dripping out of me and pushes it back in.

"I like you full of me. Leave it in there," he shrugs with a devilish smile.

"Fine, but you have to help me up then," I start, but before I say more, he's scooping my body up from the table and walking up the stairs to the bathroom.

Without a word, he leans me on the sink's edge and starts the bath, pouring a lavender liquid in the warm water. I close my eyes and inhale, letting the scent that wraps around me calm every nerve in my sore body. My exhaustion starts to set in, but he sits me in the tub with him behind me so he can caress my muscles and I can't help but smile with my entire heart. Every part of me feels whole, especially the part that feared I'd lost him forever.

When we go to my room, grateful and sated, I fall asleep with his arms wrapped around me, his kiss on my hair, and his dragon tattoo pressed against my back.

# Chapter Thirty-One

## Clif

I know I heard something. Sonnet and I are curled into each other in her bedroom after one of the strongest orgasms of my life, but I know I'm not awake because I want to be. As soon as I hear the booted footsteps going up the stairs, I shake Sonnet with my hand over her mouth to wake her up too. With one look at my face, her brows crease in concern. When she hears the noises upstairs too, her eyes widen and any bit of her sweet dreams vacate.

Sliding out of the bed and quickly slipping on the clothes from her bedroom floor, I hold her behind me as we creep up the stairs to attempt a run to the front door. I don't know who the fuck is in this house in the middle of the night, but I know for a fact it's not with good intentions. It's to catch us off guard. A true coward's move, or one of a hitman that wants to make the job a quick in and a quick out. Regardless of their plan, ours is to get the hell out of the house.

As soon as we reach the top of the stairs, the front door is in view and I turn to look at her. The footsteps above us have stopped, so I'm hoping they're distracted up there to give us the few seconds we need.

I don't even reach for the keys. We could just get to Kathy's house next door. She'd seen me enough now to know Sonnet and I are together. When her eyes meet mine, we share a nod and make a speedy dash to the door. I barely touch the doorknob when Sonnet's scream is muffled behind the thick fingers of a masked man in all black.

Whoever he is, he doesn't look familiar to me off hand. He's tall, and compared to her petite frame, he looks like he could do fatal damage to her without anything other than his gloved hands. His arms are wrapped around her, one over her mouth and the other tightly around her midsection. She's kicking and shaking her head, but she stills when he holds a gun with a silencer pointed directly at my face. We *both* still at that. I can see her eyes fill with fearful tears and right now, I'd give anything to take it away. I raise my hands in a motion to show I don't have anything on me. I'm in nothing but gray sweatpants and didn't grab anything to defend us, but at the moment I wonder if it would have even done any good if I had.

"Ok, ok. What do you want," I ask him calmly and I can see Sonnet shaking in his hold. "I can get you money."

"Clifton Wallace," the man chuckles and I go cold. "I don't want your fucking money. You owe me a life."

I'm confused until he pulls the mask off of his face and the uncanny resemblance hits me like a truck. He looks like a carbon copy of TJ only older. Fuck.

"He was your brother," I say out loud without realizing it. As soon as the words are made solid, Sonnet closes her eyes in dread and a tear escapes. She trembles in her sleep shorts and tank, and I don't think I've ever been more terrified in my entire life. He's here to collect a blood debt.

"I was going to show you how it feels to lose family. I got cousins inside, but then I hear your baby brother was transferred to solitary until his court date for the appeal. You can't just kill my fucking blood and get away with it," he snarls, spitting when he says the last bit and he looks like a rabid dog. "A life for a life."

"TJ and I fought like men. He made the deal. I didn't have a choice, I swear. I tried to get out of it," I admitted, hoping he would at least chill the fuck out when he learned that it wasn't on purpose. It was self defense.

"Why would you take that deal?" he asks, tightening his grip on Sonnet as she desperately tries to pull her tank back in place when his hold makes it ride up to reveal her stomach. "What was worth my brother's life to you?"

"He took something. I needed to get it back. I tried to give him money for it, but he wanted to fight instead," I offer, but when he looks at me, I know that isn't enough to satisfy him. "A family heirloom. It was a watch, ok?"

"The watch..." he said as he contemplated and then suddenly something clicked. His expression changed to rage and disgust. "The watch he got from *her*. He told me about a gold watch. So, this is *your* fault."

When he looks down at Sonnet, every single bit of vitriol is directed at her and I don't know what he's thinking. I try to keep his attention on me, anything to keep him talking to me, but it's too late. He's already formulating his decision and I know whatever it is, I'm going to have to find a way to stop him before it changes everything forever between us.

"You took everything from me, Clifton. I want you to watch me take what you love from you until there's nothing left of her," he spits as he keeps the gun on me, but rips a strap from her tank top. Her scream at the fabric burn on her skin combined with her exposed breast makes bile race to my throat because I know now what he's going to do…and what he's going to make me watch.

When he sees my reaction and the tear finally fall from my eyes, he smiles a yellowed grin at me as he roughly paws at her chest. Her eyes pinch closed, trying desperately to transport herself from this and what he has planned for her. I take an instinctive step forward and he fucking shoots the floor at my feet. The moment the round is discharged, Sonnet's eyes fly open and I see in her expression the moment she relaxes her muscles and gives into her fate…for me. To keep me alive. Again.

Dragging her by her messy copper hair into the kitchen, he throws her to her knees on top of the clothes strewn on the floor from when we'd made love hours earlier. Still holding her hair to control her head, he makes her look at me and I want to die. If I knew it would save her from this, I would let him shoot me in the fucking face. She winces from the pain, and I can see her hands palm to the floor for balance.

"Hey, Little Red, we're gonna show your limp dick boyfriend over here how well you suck cock aren't we?"

"P-Please don't," she cries, trying desperately to plead for him to stop, but he's already set on whatever his plan is, and the only way out is if I try to rush him for the gun. He laughs at her plea and releases her hair for a split second to backhand her roughly across her cheek. The force knocks her all the way to the ground and I swallow the vomit in my throat.

"Baby, look at me. Keep looking at me," I say softly to her doing the only thing I can with a gun pointed at my forehead. She turns at the sound of my voice and there's a connection that reinforces our love. "I got you, ok? I love you."

At the sound of encouragement, and the sight of what our shared gazes convey, he roars at the betrayal to his intentions. Leaning down, he yanks her back to her knees. Undoing his belt with one hand, he unzips his jeans and fights to take himself out, but something catches my eye at her side. A slight silver glint under the kitchen light on the floor in her hand. In a moment, everything becomes clear, and I look at my dragon queen with unbounding allegiance and admiration as I understand the fierce look in her eyes.

"I'm going to turn you into a worthless used up whore. That's all he'll see when he looks at you. Every hole you have will bleed when I'm done. Now, open your fucking mouth, Red," he snarls as he takes his less than average cock out.

She opens her mouth, but smiles up at him. He barely has a second to register the confusion before she holds my pearl handled knife up and stabs it directly into his groin. When he screams out in shock, I rush him and redirect the gun as two rounds hit the kitchen ceiling.

"Run!" I yell at Sonnet. But she doesn't get up to run. She sits up taller and stabs repeatedly into his thighs, groin, and midsection as blood begins to spray her in a red-stained baptism.

His grip on the gun loosens, and he stumbles back. When he falls hard on his ass, the look of sheer unadulterated terror on his face is warranted as my bloody dragon queen crawls over to him through the red pools on the white floor. Reaching him, she raises her hand and stabs him directly in the chest once. Twice. Three times. And then I lose count as she returns the fear he gave her back to him tenfold. By the time she starts to slow down, his black shirt shines from how soaked it's become, and I wonder if there's more blood inside his body or out of it at this point.

He gargles and coughs, more blood sputtering out of his mouth as Sonnet tilts her head while she watches, her face stone. I lean down next to her and put a hand on her back, offering her comfort, but not knowing if she needed me to avoid touching her for a while. Watching her reaction, her shoulders release a little tension and she turns to look at me. We share a moment of nonverbal deep eye contact, and I can sense our breathing sync and slow. A cough from the creep on the floor shakes her peace and she looks to me as if to tell me she has to finish this. I nod, understanding completely.

With her left hand laced with mine to offer my support, she uses her right to tightly grip the handle of my knife. When she turns her head back to him, the softness she reserved for me has drained from her face. Her eyes are dark, and all I can think of is that the type of hardness she's showing isn't born - it's made. Then I suddenly despise Gloria Franklin even more for making her feel like she had to fight for the unconditional love every kid fucking deserves. As his eyes meet hers, an acceptance washes over him as she surprises us both and slices a savage deep line across the entirety of his throat.

# Chapter Thirty-Two

## Sonnet

I've killed two people. Two. I keep waiting to feel regret or remorse, but right now I don't feel much of anything. I'm numb. When I watch the last proof of life leave the intruder's dark eyes, I inhale like I've just cleared my sinuses and can breathe freely. Clif is still holding my hand, and a small part of me is scared to look at him after he watched me slit someone's throat. If this changes the way he looks at me, I think that will hurt me worse than anything, but when I turn, nothing has changed.

"Clif," I say as the gravity of what happened crashes into me, and unwanted flashbacks start playing in my head that begin to turn my stomach. When we latch onto each other in a tight embrace on the floor, he pets my bloodied hair and kisses my temple.

"Are you ok, baby?" he asks genuinely, leaning back to inspect me for injuries, but every drop of blood I'm wearing isn't my own.

"What do we do?" I wonder out loud as I let his gaze center me. I may have gotten away with what happened to my mother, but there's no way around what this kitchen looks like. This scene doesn't look like self defense. It looks like a massacre.

"I call Walt. TJ was his. He should know his former employee had inside men and maybe still does. I'm going to get my phone, ok baby? Come here," he scoops me up and sits me on the kitchen table. Tying the strap of my tank top together to return it to my shoulder, he kisses where the small red burn still stings before running back downstairs for his phone.

I sit on the table and stare down at the asshole who assaulted me, and I flip him off with both hands. I know he can't see me because he's dead, but I don't care. He deserves not one iota of peace, in this life or the next. Within minutes Clif is coming up to me with new clothes. He didn't have as much blood on him, but he's already swapped sweats and thrown on a t-shirt.

"Walt should be here any second," he says with a reassuring tone and I let him pull a hoodie over my blood-speckled hair.

He stands between my legs and with a hand behind my head, and guides my ear to his chest to block the view of anything but him. With one hand rubbing slow circles on my back, he uses the other to hold the spot where my neck meets my head, knowing it's one of my favorite calming motions. If I close my eyes, I'm almost able to block out everything that happened tonight, but the smell of blood lingers heavily in the air like fog.

When I hear the front door, Walt and a woman enter, walking straight into the kitchen to meet us. I hear the whistle he lets out before I see him, and it's the first time I'm able to put a face to the name. He doesn't look like I thought he would. He's older, maybe 70-something, and I'm surprised he has a wife. Girlfriend? Mistress? Who knows, but for a sketchy man with a thick midsection whose aura is probably just cigar smoke, she's stunning and so very clearly out of his league - and age range.

Looking at us, the state of the man on the floor propped up against the cabinets, and the Pollock painting I'd made of the kitchen, Walt and his female companion don't seem to be in shock. She seems more focused on the house itself, taking in the interior design like she's at an open house and not the scene of a slaughter. She steps over the body with her black stilettos, looking down at him with disgust and approaches me like a concerned parent.

"We'll get you cleaned up, дорогая," she whispers to me in a beautifully thick accent I can't place, but I look to Clif for direction. "Come on, let the men talk."

"I'm staying," I say firmly while I hold Walt's gaze. He nods as I motion to Clif. "Anything you say to him, you say to me too."

"I like her," the woman remarks with a canary-eating smile while she walks back over to Walt. Instead of standing next to him though, she leaves the kitchen as she speaks over her shoulder on the way out. "I'll show myself around, yes?"

"Go on, Eva," Walt tips his head to motion to her, but she's already gone. When he looks back to the body on the floor and then to us, he sighs before bringing his attention to me. "Quite the mess you've gotten in, Red, huh?"

"None of this would have happened if you hadn't robbed me fucking blind," I snipped, unable to help myself. The chain of events were clear, and robbing me took the watch which in turn caused TJ's death and everything after. Walt's brows shot up and he smirked.

"Alligator blood in this one. I like that. No wonder Clifton here wanted to keep you to himself," he chuckles and nods his head like everything is coming together. Clif holds me tighter, like he's bracing us for whatever might come next.

"I called you because we need a cleaning crew or whatever you call it. TJ was yours and he caused this, so I thought you could, you know, make it go away," Clif explains, using his head to motion to the kitchen's blood-stained linoleum floor.

"What did you call me?" I ask, narrowing my eyes at Walt. I can feel Clif's grip tense like he's nervous that I'm talking back, but I want to know.

"I said you *had* alligator blood, Red. It's a compliment we use at my tables. One that's reserved only for those who you can't kill or rattle easily, and stay calm no matter what you throw at them. Seems like you got it in spades," Walt answers with nonchalance. Looking at Clif, he continues. "So you think what? Call me and I do this job for free? Come on, kid, you can't be that dense."

As I open my mouth to smart back at him for not even offering to help fix a problem he had a major hand in causing, Eva returns to the kitchen. Putting her manicured hand on Walt's shoulder, she flicks her long black hair back as she whispers something in his ear. I try to read the way her sharp jawline moves for a hint of what she's saying, but I can't make anything out. I slide off the table and stand at Clif's side, straightening my spine with the newfound knowledge that this guy may actually think of me as something other than the scared little girl I might look like upon first glance. It's a new feeling, to be seen differently for the first time, and I don't exactly hate it. Before I can ask what's going on, Eva stands next to him and they both level their gazes at me.

"What?" I ask, feeling like the only person in the room who's unaware of an obvious secret. Clif laces his fingers with mine, regardless of the dried blood that still crusts my hands. Eva nudges Walt, and with a slight edge to his tone, he finally lets me in on it.

"Eva here seems smitten with your mother's house. She wants it. I-"

"-I'm not *giving* you my fucking house," I snap. Walt's hands go up to signal that he's not finished. I close my mouth and sigh as Clif moves behind me to wrap his arms comfortably around my waist. I don't know why, but just like magic, with my back resting against him I feel relaxed and ready to listen. *Damn his sorcery*, I muse to myself.

"Knock off thirty from the asking price and you can sell it to her right now as is," he explains. His dress shoe kicks the leg of the corpse on the floor. "Including this...unusual decor that my crew will have to remove to redesign. I'd also suggest you two find another place to be. TJ caused quite an unrest in my ranks, and I'm not in the business of offering protection. Do we have a deal?"

"She sells you the house and we're square?" Clif jumps in to clarify. He has experience dealing with Walt and his shady bargains, so for once, I'm not going to mind a man speaking up in my place. I don't know what kind of unspoken fine print could exist in a situation like this, so I listen and wait for the details to be laid out while I flex the caked brown blood on my hands out of the cracks in my skin.

"I'm going to need all of your clothes in a trash bag left here. You shower and pack. Go to a hotel and we'll deal with the paperwork tomorrow, but I'm not risking you two leaving a trail of DNA for anyone who's a little too curious. Capisce?"

When the conversation dies down, I can tell everyone in the room is waiting for me to agree to the terms. Clif rubs my upper arms, silently reminding me that he's ok with whatever I choose and that we're in this together. Eva looks at me with a stone cold expression, but behind her green eyes, I can see the tiny flicker of hope. Walt looks like he's impatient, but also anxious to give Eva what she demands of him. With a deep breath, I make my decision.

"Deal," I say confidently and hold my hand out to them. Eva wrinkles her nose at the unclean palm I've presented her, but Walt firmly grasps it without hesitation.

"Then it's done. Drop your clothes in a trash bag and clean yourselves up, you look like a couple of serial killers," he chuckles at us before being swept up in an excited hug and kiss from Eva.

# CHAPTER THIRTY-THREE

## Clif

As Walt and Eva exit the kitchen to allow us a little privacy, I come around to face her. Framing her cheeks with my hands, I look into her eyes in awe. She has been through so much, even starting when she was just a fucking kid, and she made it out on the other side. I move my thumbs to collect her tears, but there aren't any. She searches my eyes, for what I don't know, but I respond to her silent questioning with a kiss to her soft lips.

"You good, Killer?" I ask quietly, speaking the words into her mouth before she has a chance to pull back. She nods and a dreamy haze drifts over her gaze. I know that look. She must be exhausted, but like me, thankful to finally see the end of this shit. "Show me where to find the trash bags and I'll help us out of all this so we can get cleaned up, ok? You want to take a nice long hot shower with me?" She practically purrs at the idea as her lips curl into a relaxed but closed smile.

"Under the sink," she answers blissfully while I'm sure she imagines how the steaming water will feel on her overworked muscles.

I know she's not exactly happy yet, she's just relieved and exhausted. I'm sure the idea of a hot shower sounds like heaven to her. Shit, it sounds that way to me too and I can't wait to care for her in every way I can while we wash away everything that ties us to this life so we can move on. She tilts her head in a nod to the right toward the sink, and I kiss her forehead before dropping to my knees to open the cabinet doors.

I try not to be the stereotypical guy that asks for help to find something that's right in front of my fucking face, but at first glace, I don't see trash bags anywhere. There's random plastic bags from several different grocery stores, cleaning supplies, dishwasher detergent, and so many other small boxes I'm struggling to see behind them. Figuring that the house is only hers for one more night, I don't worry about the mess as I start to dig a little. Finally, seeing the box that has a picture of flowers and a trash bin on the front, I reach for it only to have it topple over and knock a few other boxes down. Pulling the box of trash bags out and putting them on the floor behind me, I start to pick up the other boxes that fell when one in particular catches my eye.

Narrowing my eyes at the box, I try to make sense of everything at once. I'm staring directly at a box...of rat poison. From what Sonnet told me, her mother tried to kill her by mixing that in her food, but she also said that she found out by seeing the box in the trash. How many boxes of rat poison does one person usually have? Either she has a stash of these...or Sonnet never saw it in the trash. My mind races as I pick up the box, unable to curb the urge to feel how full it is. It's unopened. Maybe Sonnet thought she saw it, but she didn't.

When I turn to her, she's staring directly at me and watching my mind race as every thought is written across my face. She takes a step closer, and I tense. I don't mean to, but when she registers the movement, she stops.

"Sonnet," I say softly. It's not a question, but at the same time it is. I need her to tell me what the fuck is going on or if I'm making something out of nothing. I could be making her relieve horrible flashbacks of the worst night of her life, and I don't want her to shut me out or run from me. There's also the nagging thought in the back of my mind that there's a strong possibility she murdered her mother in cold blood, and I caught her when I jumped in her car. I'm hoping there's a healthy fucking medium here as a worst case scenario, like maybe she forgot in all the trauma or whatever the psych books say.

"I didn't plan it," she offers, keeping her feet planted like she thinks I'm going to spook easily. "I came home from work, and she laid into me like usual. Her dementia made her less filtered, but that night she told me she wished I died, that I don't deserve this life," she explains without panic or anxiety. It's like she's just talking about the weather until she breaks.

It almost feels like I'm spellbound. I can't move. I just watch her as she closes her eyes and a tear finally falls. I can tell whatever she's remembering is still hurting her, but I need to know the rest of what happened that night. When she continues, she keeps her eyes shut, like she needs to hide for the courage to tell me the rest. Walt and Eva must be upstairs because I don't hear anything here except her breathing.

"I tried to tune it out, but she slapped me and spit in my face. I turned to walk away, but she pulled my hair and told me that my dad had asked her for an abortion because he never wanted me. She said she wished she would have been strong enough to kill me before I was born," Sonnet says as her voice cracks. "I snapped. I dragged her into that garage and threw her in the trunk to shut her up, but then I came in and cleaned up and when I looked around, it was so peaceful. I got to see what life would be like without her and I was so tired that I passed out. When I woke up, I didn't remember what happened until

I got to my car and the keys were on the floor near the trunk. When I popped it, I saw her and I did the only thing I could think of. I just acted like she left."

She finishes her story - the real story of what happened that night. With the truth hanging in the air around us, she waits as she eyes me for clues as to what I must be thinking. For a second, I don't know what the fuck I'm thinking. My mind races with everything, and then suddenly it stops abruptly when I take in her image in a new light.

Sonnet stands there swimming in my black hoodie, her bare legs painted with red blotches of blood, her hair tangled, and a red hand-print on her face from the assault. At first glance, you'd think she's a tiny damsel that would hide at the first sight of trouble and is in desperate need of saving. But, my girl? The Sonnet Elizabeth Franklin I see in front of me is a warrior. She's survived shit that would have crippled even the toughest assholes I know.

I grip the trash bags in my hand as I stand up and walk to her. She takes a step back instinctively, but her backside meets the kitchen table. I hear her breath catch as I meet her, our toes touching on the floor. Putting the trash bags on the table, I raise her chin with two fingers to bring her eyes to me. She tries to avoid them, but eventually gives in and I can see the effort on her face to prepare herself for the worst.

"Do you remember the ending to book 4?" I ask her, moving my hand to run my fingers through her hair.

"W-what?" she asks with a stutter in a meek voice which I'm sure is from using all of her energy to hold it together.

"When Joey would read that series to me, my favorite was when he got to the end of book 4," I say, tilting her head back farther as I step into her closer. When our lips are almost touching, I can hear her breath pick up as I explain why it matters. "Althea didn't wait to inherit the throne from her evil mother...she took it. The Dragon

Princess only became the Dragon Queen by blood, and just look at you, baby. You're *her*. You're my queen."

She breaks out into a sob as I claim her lips with every bit of worship and want that I have, as if I can transfer it to her through a kiss. She throws her arms around my neck and kisses me back intensely. Pulling off our clothes, we leave them on the floor as I scoop her up into my arms to carry her back to the shower to show her exactly how royalty should be treated.

# CHAPTER THIRTY-FOUR

## Sonnet

It's been a week since the last night we ever spent in that house. The night he watched as I ran his switchblade over a man's throat, and the night the truth about my mom surfaced. I cashed in all of my PTO at work and put notice of immediate resignation stating the need to handle family affairs out of state, and we signed every paper necessary to sell the house to Walt and Eva. Let's face it, Walt's name might be on those papers, but he'll always be a guest in what will definitely feel like Eva's house.

Clif got rid of his apartment and we chose a small boutique hotel three hours away from it all just to think through our next steps, while still staying close enough to see Joey as he goes through the appeals process. I can't wait to meet him when he's out, which sounds like it'll be within the next year or less. Clif tells me that he's already told Joey all about me and that he can't wait to meet me either. Apparently, Joey is taking credit for Clif being able to use fantasy books to hook me into the family. He might be right.

Hearing the ocean through the open window of our hotel room, I stretch my arms over my head letting the white sheets slip down to my waist. I've never slept so sound as I have the past seven days wrapped in Clif's body and not worried about anything. I know we'll have to get back to working and house hunting soon, but for now, this break from everything we've been through has given me the peace I always wished for.

As soon as my breasts feel the ocean breeze, they're covered in the warmth of Clif's mouth while he alternates saying good morning to each nipple. I close my eyes and bask in the weightless feeling of ecstasy while he rolls on top of me, nudging my legs open so he can settle his body between them. Caging me in with his arms on either side of my face, my eyes are drawn to his chest where the dragon emblem sits over his heart.

When he leans down to nudge my nose with his, I smile at the simplicity of loving someone for who they are and receiving that back for the first time in my life since my dad was alive. His eyes meet mine, and I'm happy to drown in those beautiful blue pools as his hand slides down my side and right to my center. I melt at the look he wears when he finds me already wet for him. I can't help it. No matter how many times we make love or what positions we've contorted ourselves in, my body can't stop priming itself for another round with him.

Gliding his fingers up and down my dripping slit, he slowly parts my lips to dip inside me. I already know what he'll do next, but my body still reacts the same when he pulls them out to bring them to my mouth and wait. Opening and sticking my tongue out, he watches closely as I lick over his fingers and suck my arousal right off of them. His eyes almost roll back when he sees my cheeks hollow at the suction, and I try not to smile at how fun it is to drive him wild. The best part is, it's cyclical. I turn him on, and that turns me on, which turns him on, and so forth. It's one big turn-on-a-thon that I never want to end for as long as we live.

He uses his fingers to pull my mouth open and replaces them with his tongue as he kisses me so deeply I swear I could climax from it alone. Rolling his hips, I feel the warm head of his cock at my entrance, and I moan at the way his body feels against me. I angle myself to take him, but he pulls back from the kiss and holds himself above me.

"I love watching you take me, Little Killer," he says softly as he stares down at where he's teasing me. "The way your pretty pussy stretches…"

His words trail off as we both watch him thrust inside me in one slow motion, burying himself completely to the hilt. My mouth opens in a gasp as I try to control my breathing, but the moment he pulls out just to repeat the movement, I can't keep it quiet. With the sound of casual beach goers walking by the window, I thank whatever deities are out there that we're on the second floor.

"Fuck, Clif," I pant, trying desperately to rock my hips in an effort to convince him to fuck me faster, but he doesn't give in. In fact, he smiles and shakes his head at me and I'm reminded how much I love it when he's in control. I pout playfully, jutting out my bottom lip. He responds by leaning down and capturing it with his teeth before locking me back into a deep kiss that has my toes curling.

He slides in and out of me so slowly that it feels like every single nerve in my body is sparking. Each thrust is delivered with a controlled roll of his perfect body, and his patchwork tattoos move like ocean waves over his skin. A sheen of sweat coats both of us as we cruise closer and closer to our delicious destination. The rise and fall of our chests increase and sync, bringing us right to the edge and all I want to do is plummet into the euphoric abyss of pleasure with him over and over.

"Put your hands above your head, baby. Let me see all of you move with me inside you," Clif demands, and in this moment, he could ask anything of me and I'd gladly give it without question. I raise both hands over my head and he holds my wrists together in a single grip while his other hand pinches my clit. Crying out from the sinful shock that vibrates through me, I hold my breath for the total body high I know is coming.

"I love the way you fuck me," I happily admit when I release and exhale. It comes out louder than I intended, but at this point, I don't give a shit who hears us. We're complete strangers to everyone in this town, and it feels incredible to know we're starting fresh. He practically growls at the words coming from my lips.

"And I love the way your pussy squeezes me when you come. Show me, Killer. Come for me," he says, his thumb circling my clit faster as he loses his own fight for speed, increasing the motion of his hips. I feel it building from my core and radiating through my limbs. His hold on my wrists tightens as we both get closer. As his eyes roll back and his brows crease, he gives me the command that makes me erupt. "Come all over my cock, baby. Make a mess of me."

I don't even get the chance to say a word before he follows my orgasm with his own, both of us vocalizing our pleasure and riding the aftershocks with him still inside me. As his erection fades slightly, I can feel the liquid proof of our love start to drip out of me. Clif notices it too and pulls out slowly to keep me comfortable as he sits back to stare directly at my spread legs. Not even fighting the urge to cover up, I bring my arms down and let the pins and needles sensation ebb and flow through my hands.

"Looks like you made a mess of me, Jack," I tease as he smirks, and I do something I know will drive him crazy enough to want round two. Running my hand down my breasts, he sharply inhales when I bring my fingers to the mixture of our cum dripping out of me. Using my first and middle finger, I scoop under as much of the arousal as I can and slowly push it back inside of me as deep as I can go. Repeating the motion slowly, I continue to pump his cum back into my pussy, letting the sound of it fill the silence. I don't even think he's breathing, but when I look down, he's hard as a rock again and I smile like the evil queen he's made me.

"Keep doing that and I'm going to fuck you again, Killer," he threatens playfully, his hand going to his length to stroke himself while he watches me.

"You really think you could go again?" I taunt, knowing damn well even if he was exhausted, he'd try.

"I could play with that pretty pussy forever," he says, but his eyes warm and look at me. Pulling my hand away from my core, he brings my fingers to his mouth. They're still covered with us both, but he sucks them in before hooking the back of my neck to bring up to his lips. "Would you let me do that?"

"Let you what?" I whisper breathlessly into his lips.

"Let me fuck you for the rest of our lives. I love you, Sonnet. Let me keep you. All of you," he says with his whole heart.

"I love you too. I'm yours, Clif. All of me. Don't ever stop," I promise and beg at the same time. At my words, he pulls me onto his lap, impaling me on him in one smooth motion.

It didn't take us long to decide where to settle down and how to design our new place. Clif took a job in town with a construction company, and I jumped onto the schedule at the hospital. With the area being a lot less populated, I was able to avoid working the overnight shift so Clif and I could spend more time together.

Once Joey's case was dismissed, he was released, and I finally got to meet him even though I'd seen him in court. Clif was absolutely right. We instantly felt like family, which we officially were soon after when Clif and I woke up one morning and decided it was a great day to go to the courthouse. It feels amazing to have a life I never thought I'd find. Married to a gorgeous man I can't keep my hands off of, living in our dream cabin just like we talked about, and funny enough, we're self publishing our first fantasy novel this year about a warrior king and queen that will stop at nothing to defend their kingdom.

With every day we spend together, I'm reminded more and more that love is not always something you are granted. Sometimes it's only found in the rubble of a life you burned to the ground by dragon fire.

# *Epilogue*

## Clif, Four Years Later

Celebrating the release of our second book, now that we're officially signed with one of the biggest publishing houses for fantasy series, Sonnet and I cuddle into each other around the bonfire. Our three Great Dane rescues, Drogon, Syrax, and Meleys, are curled at our feet as they chew on the bones Joey and his fiance brought as gifts.

The sounds of the fire crackling and the wind rustling through the trees serve as white noise behind the conversations and bottles being popped open one after the other. We might have been excited for our book deal, but we're not the only ones with a cause for celebration. Looks like I'm also about to be an uncle.

"I'm really glad we finally got to meet you, Emilia," Sonnet beams. She may be a little buzzed, but she's always excited to meet another girl that she can talk about books with. "Joey said you love to read and I knew we were going to be the best sister-in-laws ever."

"Oh hell yeah, I feel like ever since my hormones kicked up, the type of romance I read is so much more...interesting," she laughs with a hand over her swollen belly. She mentioned being due in four months and they decided to keep the gender a surprise until the delivery. "Last one I read was about the kraken and it was so fucking *hot*." Sonnet and Emilia laugh, and Joey rolls his eyes playfully in return.

"Sounds like Joey's just threatened by a man who could hold his breath underwater for longer than five seconds and doesn't have to pinch his nose when he cannonballs," I tease through my slightly inebriated sense of humor.

"Dick," Joey laughs and throws a bottle cap at my face, hitting me in the forehead before falling into my lap.

"How did you guys meet again? I can't remember if you've told us," Sonnet asks as she settles back into me on the swinging bench. I inhale the smell of my wife's hair and kiss the top of her head, thanking the universe and whatever else is out there again for bringing us together. I do it at least once a day, but it never feels like enough.

"Oh my god, it's actually a crazy story," Emilia starts, smiling at Joey who looks back at her like she's an angel walking on earth. When I make eye contact with Joey, he chuckles.

"You know what, sweetheart, I think these two definitely have us beat," my brother says, finally laughing out loud and nodding his head in our direction.

When he laughs, it becomes contagious as Sonnet and I join in. Emilia looks from her fiance over to us, and Joey shrugs, taking a big gulp of his beer. Sighing, I look to my wife, who is the natural storyteller between the two of us. She did most of the writing for our book, but I was happy to provide a few ideas, mostly for what she calls the "spicy scenes".

"Fuck it," I say to her matching Joey's shrug. "If she's going to join the family, might as well..." Sonnet smiles widely with excitement and Emilia leans forward in her seat while Joey rolls his eyes as we induct her and our unborn niece or nephew into our crazy origin story. She might not even believe us, but it doesn't matter. I shake my head as my queen starts to tell the story that changed our lives and gave me the greatest adventure I could have ever wished for.

"Well, one night after I was looking around for my poor mother who wandered off, I stopped at a gas station for snacks..."

I smile at the theatrics, and pinch her side when she plays up the good girl act she met me with. She giggles and puts a finger to her lips, shushing me so I don't spoil the many surprises. I down my beer and pop the cap on the next one, waiting for Emilia's reaction when Sonnet gets to the good part in the trunk that scared the shit out of me over five years ago.

Watching her bring our story to life against the backdrop of the modernized cabin in the woods we wished into existence somehow still causes me to pinch myself. I'd never believe the story either. And to think, this all started with a shitty hand of poker, a watch that doesn't tick, and a pint-sized princess with alligator blood in her veins.


### *The End*

# Thank You

Thank you so much from the bottom of my heart for taking a chance on my debut novel. If you enjoyed it and would like to leave a review, it would mean the world to me. Reviews help indie authors like me continue to do what we love.

I'm grateful for every moment you spend with my characters and I can't wait to bring you more stories. Thank you!

# Acknowledgements

To my chosen sisters, Gretchen and Krista. You're my family and having you in my life has filled a void in my heart that I didn't know could be healed. Thank you for being the honest springboard that I could bounce ideas, vent sessions, dream cast photos, and countless Tiktoks off of. Together, we make quite the coven and we'll try our best to use our powers for good...mostly.

To my beta readers and editors, THANK YOU. You've helped immensely to make this project a polished little gem from my imagination, and for that I'm eternally grateful. Your time, feedback, and care helped give Sonnet and Clifton a happy home in the pages. I know they're just as thankful to you as I am that they can share their story without my never ending collection of run on sentences.

To my dearest friends and coworkers (who were essentially captives), thank you for listening to me talk about my writing and book ideas incessantly. It means a lot to me that you asked for updates, sneak peeks, and beta copies. The more you showed interest, the more excited I got to write, and that kept me going when I had bouts of imposter syndrome with a side of writer's block. Thank you so very much.

And to the readers, thank you for giving Sonnet and Clifton a chance, but more importantly, thank you for giving me a chance. The book community has given me friendship, encouragement, support, and confidence to share my stories. This was my debut, and it means a lot that you gave me this opportunity to be the storyteller I have always dreamed of being.

# About the Author

A lifetime avid reader, India has always dreamed of bringing her own stories to the world, doing so with her debut novel "Alligator Blood". When she's not busy working or on an adventure (either in person or in a Dungeon & Dragons campaign), you can find her on the couch cuddled up in her Ghostface fleece blanket watching disturbing horror movie marathons and eating enough snacks for an entire kindergarten class.

Follow for updates, memes, and chaos:
Tiktok: @Indiavanebooks
Instagram: @Indiavanebooks